Jasmine

The Enchanted Journey Book Two

ROSA LEE JUDE

JASMINE
The Enchanted Journey Book Two
By Rosa Lee Jude

Copyright © 2015 Rosa Lee Jude
Published by Ink On My Fingers Publishing
All Rights Reserved
Cover & Book Design by Cassy Roop / PinkInkDesigns.com
Printed in the United States of America

ISBN-10:194299401X
ISBN-13:978-1-942994-01-5

Rosa Lee Jude

Visit my website at www.RosaLeeJude.com

Books by Rosa Lee Jude

The Enchanted Journey Series
TREMBLE
JASMINE
NEVERWRONG

The Legends of Graham Mansion Series
(with Mary Lin Brewer)
REDEMPTION
AMBITION
DECEPTION
SALVATION
REVELATION

Chapter One

"I WAS REALLY SURPRISED that you agreed to see me. Pleasantly surprised, but still surprised."

Tremble thought she might need to start counting the number of times Jake said 'surprised' during their date. She was sure that he had doubled the times already and they had not even ordered dinner yet. She smiled to herself as she glanced at him over the top of the menu. He looked so nervous. It was quite uncharacteristic for the self-assured jock she dated in high school.

She could not deny that saying *surprised* to describe the previous couple of weeks of her life was appropriate, albeit there were probably stronger words. Her whole world turned upside down since she learned that her life was anything but normal. Tremble Dawson had discovered that her life, the only life she knew with her parents, Andrew and Dana Dawson, was a ruse, in many respects. Tremble was actually born immortal, an enchantress from another world. She was the daughter of Queen Jasmine and King Forrest of the Kingdom of Neverwrong. Hidden at birth in the human world by Jasmine, Tremble had been raised by Andrew and Dana with a legion of guardians secretly watching over her. Jasmine entrusted her only child to two humans—two that Tremble could not imagine her existence without. Tremble had never suspected that her parents were anyone but the couple who had showered her with love and devotion. It still made Tremble's head spin to think about all the layers of secrecy that her entire existence had entailed.

Learning that her bosses, CeCe and Bridget, at her college internship were two of the main people entrusted with her care, was another eye-opening experience. It caused her to begin to question everything in her past, even the young man who nervously sat before her.

"How was your trip? You look like you got some sun." Jake Wallace sat straight and tall across from Tremble.

His question brought her back to the present. His posture was one of the first things she had noticed that evening about him. His time in the military had changed his demeanor and some of his habits. She never remembered him sitting so straight. They had dated for several years, in high school and after graduation, until he suddenly joined the Navy and disappeared from her life.

"Yes, the weather was great. We stayed at a beautiful house with quite a bit of private space around it and direct access to the beach."

"That sounds great. You said you were with some of your mother's friends?"

"Ah, yes. They are friends of my mother's. It was a girlfriends' getaway of sorts."

"Cool. My mom and her sisters do that sometimes."

The server arrived and rescued them from their nervous

conversation.

"Good evening, my name is Lenora, and I will be your server this evening. Have you had a chance to look over the menu? May I answer any questions?"

"Yes." Tremble glanced at Jake. "I believe we have. I would like to have the Chicken Marsala with wild rice and asparagus."

"Excellent choice, ma'am. May we begin your meal with a mixed greens salad with the house strawberry poppy seed dressing?"

"That sounds lovely."

"And, for you, sir?"

"I will have a rib eye steak, medium rare, with the grilled vegetables and potatoes au gratin. I would like a Caesar salad, please."

"Another excellent choice. I will be back with your salads and bread momentarily."

"Look at us, the grown-ups ordering dinner in a fancy restaurant."

Tremble knew she needed to lighten the mood. For all that had happened and her broken heart, she now knew that this young man sitting across from her had not left her of his own devices. He had run off and joined the U.S. Navy at the prompting of a spell cast by Laken, her main Protector. She could not imagine ever being able to explain it to him. Now, Jake seemed to have awakened from the spell. He was facing the harsh reality that he had thrown their relationship away.

"Yeah, it's a long way from those Saturday nights at Pizza Palace." Jake chuckled, but Tremble could hear the somber reflection in his voice.

"Life has changed."

"It would be nice if it could change back."

"Time travel doesn't seem to be one of my hidden talents. What about you?" Tremble looked around them to the guests at adjoining tables. She wished that she had learned the spell that could conceal their conversation from others.

"No, and I'm sure if I had the ability to travel through time, the United States Navy would have found it. They are rigorous in finding every little thing out about you that you never knew existed. They found that I was allergic to peas."

"Do you like the Navy?" Tremble thought it would be a safe topic.

"You know, amazingly, I do. I like the structure, the organization. That's probably one of the things that I liked most about sports, the discipline of it."

Tremble shook her head in agreement. She remembered those qualities in him. He was religious about his training, rising early and running before he hit the gym. He never missed a practice. He was dedicated.

"I've given it the same determination that I gave sports and it is paying off. I have had some promotions in rank and opportunities to go to special trainings. I think I can really move up in the Navy, if I decide to stay in."

"That's great, Jake. But, you once talked about going to college and becoming an engineer."

"I can do all of that while I am in the Navy. The educational opportunities are amazing."

"But, aren't you about to be deployed?"

"Oh, yeah, there is that. If I can just get past this year or two of deployment, I can get my engineering education and continue to move up."

"This deployment will be to a war-torn area."

"Yes. I really can't say anything else about the location." Jake looked around as if Navy spies might be listening.

"You will be in danger."

"Yes, that is a given. My unit will be in the action. My duties do not take me directly into combat." Jake bowed his head and absentmindedly straightened the silverware in front of him. "It's like I told my folks, I'll be fine. I'm the Man of Steel, right?" Jake gave her a big smile.

Tremble's memory flashed back to the night when Jake received the nickname. It was their junior year. Even then, the star athlete was the quarterback of their winning football team. It was homecoming night, and they were playing an especially aggressive team from a neighboring community. The rivalry was long in years and powerful in emotions. The game had been fierce. The score was tight. During the last minute of the game, Jake had chosen to run fifty yards for the final winning touchdown. He was successful. The ball was in the end zone. But not before a player from the opposing team who was literally almost twice his size had tackled him. The impact was hard. Some of the players said they heard the air leaving Jake's lungs.

In the midst of the crowd going wild from the victory, word began travelling through the stands that the star player was not moving. A doctor came onto the field. An ambulance soon followed.

"You are reliving that night, aren't you? I can see it in your eyes."

Jake's question jolted Tremble back to the present as she still saw him sprawled face down on the field.

"Yeah, I, we were all scared that you had been seriously injured."

"Well, I should have been from the way that Titan clobbered me. But, like Doc Henderson said, I'm a Man of Steel." Jake reached across the table and took Tremble's hand. "And, I will be okay overseas."

Tremble had not realized that a seed of worry had already planted itself in her mind. Despite her inclination to pull away, she allowed Jake to hold her hand. It was a comfortable memory.

"You wouldn't believe who is in my unit." Jake pulled his own hand away as the server delivered their salads and bread.

"I can't imagine."

"Carrington Baxter." Jake looked up from his salad. Tremble shook her head. "The Titan who clobbered me. He is in my unit. We're like Forrest and Bubba."

"I'm not sure if that is a comforting thought or a frightful one." Tremble let out a laugh. A hearty one from deep inside. It felt good.

"How was your date with Jake?"

Tremble opened her eyes to see Dana standing in the frame of her bedroom door. She had awakened only seconds before. Her mother seemed to have the ability to know precisely when Tremble woke up. Tremble had chalked it up to some motherly instinct in the past, but now she wondered if Dana had the power to detect her sleeping patterns.

"The date was good. Jake is the same and different."

"He's matured. He's had some serious life experiences." Dana walked over to the double windows that stood just beyond Tremble's bed. "Will you see him again?"

"Now, how would that work, Mom? Do you think CeCe could beam him to Neverwrong?" Tremble slung her feet off the side of the bed barely missing Choo Choo's head. The tiny dog jumped out of the way and burrowed under a blanket.

"I don't know. It is not for certain that you will depart immediately, is it? Have they given you a schedule?"

"Mom, here's what I have come to understand." Tremble looked at her mother's reflection in the long mirror that stood in the corner. Multi-colored sparks flew out of Tremble's hair as she briskly brushed it. She watched as Dana backed away so as not to be hit by the tiny flames.

"It's increasing in its intensity."

"It would appear so. Bridget says it is because my powers are becoming more pronounced as I learn how to use them." Tremble gave her hair a rest and drew the long black locks into a scrunchy hair band. Her fingertips glittered as she drew her hands away from the purple streaks that naturally highlighted her hair. "I have come to understand that each of these guardians appears to have either strict orders from Belladonna or their own carefully developed opinion of what I should do and when I should do it. I, however, have decided to ignore all of that. If I am the heir, then my opinion should count, too."

"Darling, I understand that you must feel out of control with your own life. But, don't forget that all of these people were carefully put into place to watch over you."

"I haven't forgotten that, but I think there is something we need to remember. Jasmine put some of this in place over twenty years ago. We do not know how much of this plan was originally hers or contrived by someone else."

"That's true. How do you think you can tell the difference though?"

"There's only one way that I can. I need to hear it from *her*." Dana turned and looked her daughter in the eyes. "Mom, I am going to go find Jasmine."

"Tremble, it's a dangerous proposition."

"I realize that it is risky. No matter what I do, there is great risk. I just feel in my heart, my soul, that this is right."

"Tell me more about what you mean by that." Dana drew Tremble to sit down beside her on the bed.

"It started on the last night that we stayed at the beach. I had this dream that Jasmine was in a deep dark forest, and she was beckoning me to come to her. I have had this same dream every night since, and I keep getting closer to her."

Tremble watched as a tear escaped from Dana's eye. Her mother quickly wiped it away and took hold of Tremble's hand.

"There are a few things that Jasmine shared with me that I have shared with no one, not even your father. You just described one of them. Jasmine said your dreams would be the way she could communicate with you. She gave me an example of her appearing in a dark forest." Dana took a deep breath. "You are right. It is time for you to begin your journey to find her. There is one thing that she said you must do. You will not like it. She knew this. You must take Laken with you."

"Mother, I feel very uncertain about him." Tremble stood up. Rays of green flowed from her fingertips.

"I understand that. Jasmine foretold it."

"Really? Then why is he my Protector?"

"Tremble, I think that as much as we may think we know at this point, there is much yet to be revealed. Jasmine said you would have a Protector and that you would not trust him. She did not indicate whether your distrust was warranted. I think she saw it as a protection of its own."

"I don't understand." The rays coming from her fingertips began to change from green to blue. Tremble was calming down.

"Distrust does not always work negatively on our behalf. It

can also serve to keep us on guard, watching everything carefully to determine what the truth really is. I think, on the surface, you should trust Laken. I think that he is sincerely dedicated to you and your safety. There may be factors influencing him that he is not aware of, so that is where you need to pay attention. He has the knowledge and skill to help you find Jasmine."

Tremble joined her mother again on the edge of the bed. It seemed to Tremble that her mother had aged a great deal in the last few weeks. All of those years of secrecy and worry now seemed to have manifested themselves with tiny lines on her mother's forehead that she had never noticed before. Tremble knew that all this revelation would have been easier on her mother if Andrew was by her side. It would have been easier for both of them.

"Okay, I will listen to what you are saying. I think that the two people who I can trust unconditionally, at this point, are you and Jasmine." Dana smiled and nodded. "I think I am going to have to leave one of you to find the other. It pains my heart and scares me to do this."

"Those are both things I feel as well." Dana pulled Tremble into an embrace. She rocked her daughter as she had done so many times in Tremble's childhood. "It is my turn to let you go and have that same trust in Jasmine that she had in me." Dana pulled back and looked Tremble in the eyes. "Before you embark on this journey, you must call upon Jasmine and tell her what you are doing. As I held you for the first time, she told me that you would always have the power to reach her. As long as she was living, she would hear you. I think your dreams give us evidence that her life force is still intact. Whisper her name and tell her your plans. I think she will help you find her."

Tremble watched as her mother rose and walked toward

the doorway. Dana hesitated a moment and turned back to her daughter.

"You didn't really answer my question about Jake. Is there still something between you? Still a spark?" The younger version of her mother reappeared in the teasing smile that crossed her face.

"You know the answer to that, Mom. You know my loving Jake was not the problem. Now that I know he didn't leave of his own accord, it makes my feelings even more jumbled." Tremble paused and thought a moment. "I really think I could tell him all about this and he would understand. He would believe me. I just do not know if it is fair to put such a burden of worry on the shoulders of a man who is heading off to war. He needs to concentrate on staying alive."

"I wouldn't sell those shoulders short, Tremble. They are strong, physically and emotionally. Your father and I knew from the beginning that Jake's love for you was true. Even when he was a teenager, his heart was devoted to you. I think you are right about his understanding. I also think he deserves to know the truth." Dana paused as she headed to the doorway. "I know you don't want to hear this, but I see the same kind of devotion coming from Laken. Do not sell him short either. His devotion is very connected to your future safety as your explore this other world."

After her mother left, Tremble pondered what Dana had said. Maybe she should confide in Jake. Perhaps, it would be the clearest test of his love and loyalty for her to tell him the most incredible thing about herself. She could always have someone teach her a memory-erasing spell if she thought the knowledge was too much for him. She was sure that the other man of devotion would relish her thinking that way. She was starting to think magically.

Chapter Two

"I HAVE REACHED a decision regarding my next plan of action."

The mood around the breakfast table was pensive and quiet. For the first time, Tremble thought she had really gotten everyone's attention. CeCe, Bridget, and Laken were her three main guardians, but they had not been accustomed to viewing her as a grown-up Royal. She was not at all thrilled to have to play the 'heir to the kingdom card.' Nevertheless, her instincts told her that she needed to have, at the very least, a slight upper hand going forward. Like many with power, she was not sure how to use it. She thought that she just might lose it, if she did not exercise it now and then.

"I think it is time that I begin to search for Jasmine." Tremble held up her hand as CeCe, Bridget, and Laken began to speak. "I realize that you do not think I am ready nor do you think she is ready to be found. Jasmine has communicated with me via my dreams. I believe she is telling me to begin."

"What do you mean via your dreams?" Laken was the first to jump into the questioning.

"It began while we were still at the beach. I have been having the same dream each night. In each of them, Jasmine gets closer to me. I think it is a sign."

The three exchanged glances. Tremble swore that they could communicate telepathically.

"Tremble, dear, I do not want to belittle what you are saying." Tremble noticed that Bridget had on pink pajamas with orange flamingos on them. A double take showed her that the flamingos were moving. "I, for one, do not think you are close to being ready for such a journey. You must still learn many things. Why, long distance travel alone is a skill that takes weeks to master, as well as—"

"Bridget, I appreciate your concern, but wouldn't you agree that time is of the essence? There's one thing that none of you seem to be thinking about." Tremble looked around the table. Each person gave her a blank stare. "My twenty-first birthday is just a couple of weeks away. This is a significant number, correct?"

All three of them nodded. Tremble could almost see the wheels turning in their heads.

"You know, we've been so caught up in her training, we've failed to remember that we are actually ahead of schedule." CeCe spoke in a soft, even tone. "None of this, including her knowledge, was supposed to begin until after her birthday." CeCe paused and her eyes locked with Bridget's. Simultaneously, they both looked at Laken. "Why did you come early? Why did the men in white jackets come early?"

Tremble laughed at CeCe's last question. "Men in white jackets, I hadn't thought of that. I shall be the inmate taking over the asylum." Only Dana laughed with her.

"Why have we not thought to question him about this before?" Bridget slid her chair back from the table. The flamingos came to a stationary state. "What are you hiding from us? What spell did you work to block this realization?"

Beads of sweat formed on Laken's perfect forehead. His tan complexion began to appear tainted by the multicolored lights that were visible under his skin. Tremble recalled from the previous time this happened that it seemed to be Laken's indicator of extreme emotion, mainly fear. He was hiding something.

"I am not supposed to reveal any information about the timing."

"Why? Why would Belladonna not want us to know? We have been part of Tremble's guardian team from the beginning. Our allegiance is tested and true. Our devotion is resolute."

Tremble could detect a growing anger coming from Bridget. It was a rare emotion for the woman. There were the outward signs of frustration that appeared on her—the clinching of her hands, the reddening of her neck—but also she began to give off a distinct odor. Tremble wondered if the others could detect it. It was not an offensive odor. In fact, the smell gave Tremble a feeling of reassurance. There was nothing phony about Bridget. She smelled of cinnamon. It conjured a feeling of healing within Tremble.

"Well, what do you have to say for yourself, nephew?" CeCe's tone conveyed anger. She would use her 'family card' to make her point. "Why has Belladonna instructed you to conceal this information?"

Slowly, Laken looked up. Dana gasped as they all saw the

change in him. His eyes glowed green, piercing emerald green. He did not seem to notice their alarm.

"It's my father. It's Forrest who has sent you early." Somehow, Tremble knew what she was saying was correct. Stunned silence surrounded her. "You aren't just governed by Belladonna. Jasmine and Forrest have the power to send you forth as well; they just have not used it. Forrest has bypassed Belladonna and Jasmine in this directive." The information just kept flowing out of Tremble. She did not know how she knew it, but she was not about to stop it. This was a revelation, an important one. "You also worked the spell on Jake to make him reappear in my life. You had not realized that by sending him off to the military, you were setting the prophecy in motion. The window of discovery has been open since then. Jake's leaving was part of the prophecy. It would take the power of love to set it in motion."

Tremble stood up and began to pace back and forth. "That's when everything started changing. None of you noticed it. It was too miniscule in its presentation. After Jake left, I went through a profound change of emotions. It was the catalyst for the emergence of my powers."

"Oh, Tremble, I had no idea." Dana stood up and began to pace. "I should have noticed."

"Mom, don't beat yourself up. First, you were dealing with your own emotions remember? It had not been long since Dad had passed away. Secondly, this change did not really start until I was in college. The first semester of my freshman year was, well, interesting."

"Interesting?" CeCe stood in front of Tremble with her arms crossed. The same stance CeCe took when one of the associates at the advertising agency voiced an idea she did not like.

"I chalked it up to too many parties with adult beverages."

Tremble chuckled, but no one else was laughing. "There are several little examples, but the biggest one occurred at a frat party. One person was coming on too strong. I pushed him away and he flew across the room." Tremble made eye contact with her mother. "I think that's why I haven't had too many dates in college. That and the sparks that fly out of my fingers."

"With the exception of your mother, mortals can't see that." Bridget's tone was very serious. "Your power has manifested itself that way since you were very young. We put a visual block on it."

"I've noticed the sparks getting more powerful and colorful as she has gotten older." Dana shook her head at Bridget.

"We thought it was important for you see these changes in her."

"And, why not Andrew?"

"Andrew would have thought her fingers were on fire." Bridget's tone changed to laughter. "Seriously, he would have wanted to fix it. It is not fixable. It is a part of her wonderfully natural ability. She will learn to control it."

Tremble turned her attention back to Laken. He had stationed himself in a chair in the corner out of the direct line of the conversation.

"You've got some explaining to do. Am I right? Was it Forrest who directed you to start the process early?"

"He said no one would figure out it was him. He said you needed the extra time."

"He underestimated his daughter." CeCe responded. "How in the world did Forrest communicate with you? Did you tell Belladonna?"

"King Forrest is very powerful, but I'm pretty sure he is confined wherever he is. I did not receive a visual of him."

"Why didn't you say anything about this when he came to me in my dream? You were the first one I confided in."

Tremble's mind raced thinking back to when they were at the beach. Laken had taught her how to extract a dream from her memory so that they could all see it. The dream was the physical representation of Andrew with what they thought was the voice of Forrest.

"Answer our questions, Laken." CeCe drew closer to him.

"Belladonna doesn't know."

Bridget gasped.

"Why haven't you told her?" CeCe walked even closer to him.

"King Forrest is surrounded by dark magic. I don't know how I can detect this, but it is the first thing I noticed."

"I don't understand what he is talking about."

CeCe shifted her attention to Tremble's question. "Everyone has an aura, mortal or immortal. Our ability, as enchanters, to detect them is distinctly in our favor. We can see them. We can feel them. You do not have to see someone to detect his or her aura. It will show up in a verbal communication as well. For the most part, Tremble, your detection of auras is blocked. You would only be able to see the strongest of physical auras, at this point."

Tremble pondered CeCe's statement for a moment. She knew that she had already detected several auras.

"I think then that I must have seen Belladonna's aura when I first saw her. It appeared to be fuchsia."

"Yes, that is correct. Belladonna's aura is primarily that lovely color. It has significantly darkened in the last few years as her responsibilities have increased. King Forrest's aura is very pure and strong. It manifests itself in clear, silver light."

"King Forrest communicated with me through telepathy. He spoke to me during one of my final days of training. He told me that I must set into motion the signs of the prophecy so that Tremble will have additional time to come to grips with who she is as well as to learn and prepare, and that I must keep this knowledge secret. The message seemed logical to me." Laken paused. His nervousness seemed to be lessening. "But, both that time and when I viewed Tremble's dream, I noticed that the aura I detected was dark green. It is very strong. I was afraid to tell this to anyone, even Belladonna."

"But, we just—"

CeCe gave Tremble a strong, direct look. Tremble heard the word 'no' in her head. The occurrence shocked her. She broke the gaze and turned away, pretending to cough. When she looked back, both Dana and Bridget were watching her.

"Did Forrest tell you specifically what you should do to set these signs in motion?" CeCe's voice was calm. Tremble thought that she sounded like a lawyer questioning a friendly witness.

"No. Belladonna told me that my appearance in Tremble's life would be preceded by the appearance of two men in white jackets. Knowing Jake's current position in the military, I thought it would be logical for his appearance to be one of them. I decided that my more subtle appearance in similar attire could qualify as well."

"That's why it looked like you were arguing with him, isn't it, CeCe? You didn't think he should be part of the sign." Tremble tried to remember everything she had seen through the glass walls of CeCe's office the first time she saw Laken.

"I assumed that his actions had been directed by Belladonna. I should not have assumed. As you know, Tremble, Laken's physical presence was not visible to mortals, at that point. He put me in an uncomfortable position by appearing in the office, especially during the presentation to our potential clients."

"What? During our presentation? I didn't see him then."

"You didn't?" Bridget joined the conversation. "He came in the room and sat right behind you."

"No, I didn't see him until after I returned from lunch."

"After you had seen Jake."

A screen appearing behind her punctuated CeCe's statement.

Tremble watched as the silent movie version of Jake's surprise appearance at Carmichael's played out on the screen. She was mesmerized as she saw this incredibly personal moment recreated before her. She noticed the nervous way that Jake kept fingering his hat. She saw his pained expression as she looked away from him.

"Oh, CeCe, did you see that?" Bridget rose from her seat and joined CeCe in front of the screen.

"Yes. Did anyone else see anything unusual?" CeCe turned around and looked individually at Dana and Laken before her gaze rested on Tremble. Dana and Laken both shook their heads negatively.

"I don't understand."

"I'm going to play it again."

Tremble stared at the screen. Everything seemed as she remembered it, with the exception of her own expressions. There appeared to be nothing in the background even that looked out of place to her. "It looks just as I remember although I can't believe that I didn't take more time with my hair that morning considering the presentation that we were—"

"Tremble, forget about your hair." With another wave of her hand, CeCe made the scene come back into view. "I want you all to view this again. When I freeze the image, I want each of you to tell me how many people you see."

The view began with Tremble sitting down and starting to

eat her salad. After a few moments, CeCe froze the image and looked around the room. "Tremble, who do you see?"

"I see a gentleman at a table behind me, a lady sitting alone beside me and two men sitting in the corner."

"The rest of you?" Dana, Laken, and Bridget all noted three people. None of them saw a man sitting behind Tremble.

"What?" Tremble stood up and walked toward the screen. "You don't see Mr. Suedama reading his newspaper? Bridget, you and CeCe, you must know him. He works in security at The James, doesn't he? I see him sitting at the welcome desk sometimes."

"CeCe, what's going on? Do you see this man?"

"I do, Bridget. I have seen him many times. I just had no idea that everyone else wasn't seeing him."

"I really don't understand. Why can you see someone that Bridget cannot?" Tremble looked back and forth between CeCe and Bridget.

"Hold that thought. I want to try something else." CeCe advanced the scene again. Jake walked up to Tremble and the conversation began.

"Oh, my! I see a man sitting behind Tremble now." Bridget exclaimed, looking back at Laken.

"So do I."

"Dana?"

"No, I still don't see anyone."

"CeCe, he must be an immortal."

"Indeed. He's not one of our forces."

"You guys are crazy. That is just Mr. Suedama. He's harmless." Tremble left her position near the screen and sat down on the coach.

"He is hardly harmless, Tremble. You asked why I could see

someone who Bridget and Laken cannot. It is because of the level of infused magical intelligence or perception that I possess. Because you are descended from The Seven, your level of magical perception cannot be hindered except by spells sanctioned by Royals above you and those who serve them, such as Bridget and myself. The Royal Family has bestowed those of us who are subjects of the Kingdom of Neverwrong with power, and our level of power is based on our role in the overall community. Obviously, those in the Neverwrong Military are given higher levels of power than say those who work in less dangerous positions. Based on your rank within the Neverwrong Military, you are given clearance to different amounts of secured information, much like the military in the human world. My rank is higher than both Bridget's and Laken's. I have been given the highest level of magical intelligence and perception bestowed on anyone outside of the Royal Family."

"I don't even think I can fully begin to grasp what you just said." Dana stood up and walked toward CeCe. "But, I believe I do understand that this means that man is dangerous."

"Yes, you are very correct, Dana." Bridget joined them. "This being is most definitely not a human man. He is also aware of the magical perception levels and possesses powers that can manipulate them up to a point."

"One of the key aspects to the beginning of the fulfillment of the prophecy is that the heir would become aware. The heir would start being able to use the magical talents more fully." CeCe made the screen disappear. "It is now obvious to me that Tremble's perception has all along been beyond what we anticipated. It is not surprising since there has never been someone who descended from two lines of the The Seven."

"When Jake arrived in a white jacket, it was the beginning of setting the prophecy into motion. That most certainly tampered with the level of magical perception 'Mr. Suedama' had created."

"So spit it out, CeCe. Who do you think Mr. Suedama is?"

"I think he is Scordato or, at the very least, a clone of him."

"A clone of Scordato! There could be more than one? Oh, this is sounding worse by the minute." A sick look crossed Dana's face.

"Scordato has the power to clone himself?"

"Most certainly, Tremble. You shall learn to do that as well, eventually. Watch this." Bridget twirled around several times as she chanted. It sounded like an old rock 'n' roll song. As she continued, it also looked like she was doing Chubby Checker's twist. It was only a few minutes before two Bridgets stood before them.

"Oh, my, word." Dana started to sit down. There was not a chair under her until Laken made one magically appear.

"Bridget One remains home base and is the controlling force behind all of Bridget Two's functions. Bridget Two can go places and do things without Bridget One being nearby or directing every thought and move, but Bridget Two cannot carry on the level of conversation or actions that the original can."

"So what would be Scordato's purpose in having a clone hang around me?"

"To gather information." Laken answered her question. "It is my humble opinion that the real Scordato could not come to this mortal world without being detected by Neverwrong security. A facsimile of him might show up as being closer to a mortal. This Mr. Suedama can probably not perform any magic other than the act of travelling back and forth. Both tasks that would be initiated by Scordato himself."

"So that means he wasn't any real danger to me?"

"Tremble, it means that your security has been compromised. We will have to inform Belladonna immediately." CeCe began walking toward the door. "Bridget, I want you and Laken to remain here until Belladonna sends additional security."

"Additional security! Why do I need more security? Mr. Suedama has been around me for months. If he wanted to do something to me, he had plenty of opportunities."

"Tremble, Scordato is a powerful force. He is bent on destroying Neverwrong as we know it." Bridget took hold of Tremble's hands as she began to speak. "But, more than that, he wants to be the Supreme Ruler of Neverwrong, and he wants to do it by fulfilling the prophecy that he created. All of these years, you have been protected because you are the precious offspring of Queen Jasmine and King Forrest, and we have grown to love you and your family."

"As time passed, we were allowed to learn more about Scordato." CeCe continued. "It became apparent that while he enjoyed holding this threat over our heads, he also wanted this scenario to play out as *he* wishes. That means he wanted you to grow into an adult and be his opponent."

"He will do whatever he has to in order to eliminate Jasmine and Forrest as secondary opponents." Laken stared off into space as he spoke. Tremble found the look on his face to be very strange. It was completely devoid of emotion. "It is you who he wants to be his final adversary."

"Why? What is so special about me?"

"He sees himself as the most powerful of all. He thinks that because he is a twin of Baldric and was the one left behind that this has given him increased powers. He has absorbed all of the ancient secrets found in the Library. Scordato has possibly sought out other magical kingdoms and learned of their powers that may be different from ours." CeCe paused a moment. Tremble broke her gaze on Laken and discretely pointed in his direction. "He created a prophecy that has in its fulfillment someone who he might consider to be his equal. The fact it worked out that you are a descendant of Perpetua and Baldric was all the better. With his identicalness to Baldric, he sees you as part him."

"Oh, that is not a pleasant thought."

"I agree. Yet, it might prove to be more valuable than you can currently imagine." CeCe began to walk toward the door. "I really must go and contact Belladonna. I believe it will be most beneficial to journey home to Neverwrong for a consultation. I will be in touch with you, Bridget, and Laken. Dana, keep your chin up. All is good. Tremble, walk out with me, I need to talk to you privately."

Tremble followed CeCe outside to the front porch. CeCe closed the door behind them. With the flick of her wrist, she put up a glowing metal shield between them and the door.

"A precaution, purely a precaution. I will be brief and to the point. I do not want to cause Laken to wonder what I am speaking about to you." CeCe took a deep breath. "I think that three of us saw the color of Laken's eyes change." Tremble nodded. "I do not think it was visible to your mother, and it is probably best that information stay unknown to her."

"Yes, I don't like to keep things from her. But, I do agree. She has too many worries as it is. I am afraid to ask what you think this means as I already have my suspicions."

"I think there is no doubt that somehow Scordato has been able to channel through Laken in some way. It is the main reason I want to talk to Belladonna face-to-face. We have to discover how this happened. Please understand me. I do not think that Laken knows this is happening. In fact, I believe that if he did, he would end his life. He is that loyal. Bridget agrees."

"Would it be like a possession?"

"I do not think so. Enchanters do not possess others. We have the power to do it, but usually only on a non-magical being. It would take a lot of energy for even someone as powerful as Scordato to take possession of a young, strong, finely tuned Protector. Laken has been groomed to be the very best."

"Should I be afraid of him?"

"No, again, I do not think so. You must always be on guard. Consider him your guardian and closest companion. Be aware, however, of moments, like today, when he is not alone. When some power has overtaken him. Tremble, honestly, we might find out that this is something that was created by Belladonna or even one of your parents. I hope to know more when I return." CeCe began to remove the shimmering shield around the door. She stopped herself. "I am going to give you one piece of advice, personal advice. I realize that up until a couple of weeks ago, you saw Bridget and me in a completely different way. Perhaps you feel distrusting of us on some level. I would understand that."

"I would not use the word 'distrusting.' I would more liken the feeling to reserved caution."

"Touché. We truly have your best interests at heart. You really earned the internship. It was a great relief to us that you did. My advice to you is personal, none of my business really. It is about Jake."

Tremble could feel her defenses rising. She might have to draw a line. "CeCe, Jake is in the past. I know that I should leave him there."

"It will surprise you to learn that both Bridget and I disagree. You need someone besides your mother to hold onto in this world. You need to have someone who you know you can trust, and love, if you are still inclined. You have my word that Jake will not be influenced in any way. He may be someone who you wish to confide in. Bridget can show you a way to do that, which will bring no harm to him, or you. She did not marry her Vietnam soldier, but he was a real part of her life, once upon a time. Think about it. It's not too late."

Chapter Three

BRIDGET ONLY NODDED as Tremble re-entered the room. She and Laken were on the couch in deep conversation. She was speaking in motherly tones. It was early afternoon and Tremble found her mother in the kitchen cleaning up some dishes.

"I am just numb." Dana did not even look up from the sink where she stood. "There are too many pieces to this puzzle."

"I totally agree. Yet, I am finding a little comfort in the knowledge."

"What do you mean?" Dana turned around with a dishtowel in her hands. She was repeatedly drying them; wringing her hands with worry was more like it. Tremble watched as her mother walked to the coffee pot, then stopped and reached into the cabinet above. "I think we need to switch to tea in the afternoons, green tea, less caffeine, the illusion of health."

"That or wine." Tremble chuckled as Dana lifted one eyebrow in consideration of her suggestion. "I am finding comfort in the knowledge, because no matter how complicated and scary it is, I am learning. You can face things much better, no matter how bad, by at least having more knowledge of your adversary."

"Quite true, wise daughter. You sound like your father. For all his anxious concern at times, he was a calming force and very methodical in his process."

"I need to talk to you, privately. Maybe we could think of some errands we need to run."

"Well, I was thinking it might be good for me to go by the medical complex. I know my staff is holding down the place fine, but there are surely some documents or bills that need my attention. Why don't we let the others fend for themselves with the deli stuff in the fridge? They seem to need to talk as well. Bridget seems concerned about Laken."

"Great idea. I am going to take a quick shower. Will you call and see if the Pet Spa has a spot for Choo Choo this afternoon? We could drop her off for some pampering."

"I will call while you are showering. Let's plan to leave in about forty-five minutes."

"WE GOT OUT OF *home jail* easier than I expected." Tremble laughed as she adjusted the mirrors on her mother's car before they left the driveway.

"Yes, I think that Bridget needed some private counseling time with Laken. He might be in magical time out."

"Your mood sure has changed from this morning."

Tremble waved to the elderly man who lived on the corner of

their block. He was walking his dog. Tremble had always thought he reminded her of someone, but she never could quite put her finger on whom. The canine caught Choo Choo's attention and she jumped up to the backseat window to bark a greeting.

"The prospect of doing something normal, even work-related, is sort of like a welcomed vacation. After we drop off the princess for her pamper appointment, let's go and eat at Bella's Café."

"Oh my, that sounds wonderful. It will give us some time to talk. Before CeCe left this morning, she talked to me about Jake."

"Really?"

"It surprised me, too. I had not thought about him even being a topic she would bring up. She said that she and Bridget had been talking and thought that I should hold on to his friendship. I think there is a story there. Maybe a mortal in the past who one of them didn't continue seeing because of the magical circumstances."

"Hmm, that is something that I hadn't considered about either of them. Your father and I saw them off and on through the years, especially Bridget. But, I never heard her mention anyone."

"Do you have any idea how old CeCe and Bridget are?"

"Not really, I just assumed that they were about my age." Dana paused as they pulled up to the pet spa.

"I'll be right back."

Despite the time that had passed since Choo Choo had visited the spa, she began wagging her tail, as she spied the owner of the business, Candi, come out to greet her.

"That was fast." Dana said as Tremble got back into the car.

"Candi had just finished up with her previous customer and was waiting for us to come. Choo Choo seemed thrilled to see her."

"She is such a caring soul. Did you know that she used to operate a very successful day care?"

"No, when was that?"

"When you were young. You stayed with her when you were very small for a while. She had to go through Neverwrong clearance."

"Oh my, that is too funny. Does she know that?"

"Not exactly, but Samantha Garland worked for her for a while to check her out, so to speak."

"It never occurred to me before it was brought up the other day that the Garlands' names were the same as the *Bewitched* family."

"It was the first thing your father noticed. He thought it was very strange. We liked them okay, but your father never connected very well with Darrin. Andrew did not trust him. Those early years were in a word—strange. Your father once joked that we should write a book. The walls must have had ears because we got a visit shortly thereafter about things we could not do. Dealing with Neverwrong guardians has been hilarious in many respects. I am glad it was not always a serious affair. Some of the guardians, like Bridget, made the process fun, at times. Overall, it has been enjoyable. Now, tell me more about the discussion concerning Jake."

"Okay. Let me see if I can remember what CeCe said. I guess I could extract that memory from my mind and let you view it on the windshield."

"That's okay, dear. I will take your second-hand version."

"I will say that all of this has helped my memory. I think I can just about remember what CeCe said, word for word. Something like this—'You need to have someone who you know you can unconditionally trust, and love, if you are still inclined. You have my word that Jake will not be influenced in any way. He may be someone you may wish to confide in. Bridget can show you a way to do that, which will bring no harm to him, or you. She did not marry her Vietnam soldier, but he was a very real part of her life, once upon a time. Think about it.'"

"Vietnam soldier?"

"Bridget told me a story when I first started my internship about her marriage to a man who had served in the Vietnam War. He came home safely. About a year later, though, he was in an accident and passed away. I asked CeCe if the story was true. She said that Bridget wasn't married, but that the soldier was very real."

"You know, it is hard to tell how old these ladies are. I'm sure they have ways to preserve whatever look they want."

"Yes, but it does make sense that they might be close in age to Jasmine."

"Yes, it does. I get the impression that they are friends with Jasmine, on some level."

Tremble pulled into the parking lot of Bella's Café. The downtown business had been a favorite of the Dawson family since it opened a decade earlier. Operated by a husband and wife, Zach and Emily, the café was named after their only daughter. It was part bistro, part eclectic artist hangout. All the food was farm-to-table using only regionally grown foods. Even the sodas that they offered were special brews created by Zach's father called Cooley's. Grapefruit was Tremble's favorite and that was the first thing she said to Emily when the woman gave her a big hug of welcome.

"I need a double grapefruit, extra crushed ice, with some limes thrown in for a kick."

"Hard day at college, my dear girl? You are a sight for sore eyes. We have missed you."

"Not near as much as I have missed you guys and your luscious food. Please tell me you have quiche today."

"We have quiche today, spinach and mushroom with white cheddar. We also have another one of your favorites, tomato basil cream soup." Emily's freckled nose squinted as she smiled. Tremble estimated that the woman must be in her mid-thirties, but her strawberry-blonde hair and slender figure gave her the look of a teenager.

"You must be psychic to have all my favorites on the only day I have been here this year. How did I get so lucky?"

"Zach looked into the crystal ball this morning and said, 'Tremble's coming.' I've learned to not doubt his crystal ball." Emily winked and laughed as she directed her attention to Dana. "And, just what would my second favorite customer like to have today?"

"I don't think I can beat Tremble's choices, except that I would like some of your wonderful coffee. Oh, and let's start with some cheese straws."

"Yum. I forgot about those."

It did not take long for Emily to return with their beverages and the appetizer. They always liked to sit at the table that was closest to the newsstand area of the shop. There were a variety of newspapers and magazines for sale as well as books by local authors. Several days a week, during lunchtime, artisans demonstrated their talents and sold their wares. From pottery and jewelry to quilts and intricate works of metal art, there was sure to be a craftsperson with an interesting story to share.

"I have missed this place. This feels like home as much as our own house does."

Tremble looked around and took in the décor of mismatched

tables and chairs with accents of art by the talented hands that displayed their handcrafted skills. The Mamas and The Papas serenaded them from an old stereo in the back.

"So, what do you want to do about Jake?" Dana had almost finished her first cup of coffee before she brought up the subject.

"I think I wish I could turn back time. I've spent almost the last three years trying to forget our relationship only to discover that the reasons we broke up weren't real."

"I never suspected that anyone had interfered, Tremble. Jake's leaving shocked me, but I just chalked it up to you two growing up and going your separate ways. I should have listened to Jake's mother." Dana smiled and nodded as Emily refilled her cup and brought Tremble a refill as well.

"What do you mean?"

"Sylvia tried to talk to me about it. You know, it was not too long after we lost your father. You were heartbroken. I did not want to listen to the mother of the reason you were unhappy. She just kept saying that the decision came out of nowhere. I just never considered that he could have possibly been influenced by these guardian forces who have shadowed our lives."

"Oh, Mom, don't beat yourself up about this. You could not have known. As shocked as I was, I myself thought that he had just outgrown whatever we had together. After the outer shell of wounds had healed, I tried to find a place in my heart to lock it away and learn from it. I imagined that he was half a world away and that I might not have to worry about coming face-to-face with him again until some far off class reunion." Tremble swirled her spoon around in the soup that Emily had placed before her. "By now, I thought my heart had learned to live without Jakeson Anthony Wallace."

"And now?"

"For a few moments the other night while at dinner it was as if no time had passed. It was as if, perhaps, he had been away on a long vacation and we were catching up. It felt familiar. It felt safe."

"Maybe that is your answer, dear. CeCe could be right. It could be a very healthy thing for you to have someone to share this grandiose adventure with who hasn't been or isn't involved with it now."

"Mom, how in the world would I even begin to tell him that I'm not who he thinks I am?"

"Tremble, you are exactly the same person he fell in love with five years ago. You just have a different heritage than either one of you could have ever imagined. What you have learned will shape how your life proceeds in the future, it will not change who you have been."

"What if he doesn't believe me? It would break my heart all over again. What if he gets mad when he learns about how he was influenced?"

"I'm sure he will not be happy to learn he was put under a spell in order to get him out of your life. He will probably have some anger with that. Frankly, I would be worried if he did not. I do not think that he will be mad at you about it. I think Jake loves you enough to open his mind to the possibility of anything, no matter how crazy it may sound. He may not understand it, at first. Do we even understand it? Yet, I think he would welcome the opportunity to have a chance with you again. Love makes us see things the way our heart wants us to."

"You two have been gone a long time."

When Dana and Tremble arrived back home, Bridget and Laken were watching out the window.

"We had quite a few errands to run." Dana's explanation ended as she and Tremble entered the house carrying several bags and packages. Choo Choo scampered in behind them with little purple bows in her hair.

"Oh, the little dog is different." All eyes went to Laken as he finished his comment.

"Yes, Choo Choo has been to a groomer. She was bathed and clipped."

"I do not understand the human obsession with dogs, or cats, or pets, period." The look that crossed Dana and Tremble's face was nothing short of outrage. "I mean, they can't even communicate with you." This time, Bridget joined them as their mouths opened in shock.

"You have got to be kidding. Surely, you have studied the human experience enough to know that what you said was just wrong." Bridget shook her head.

"Just because I have studied it doesn't mean I agree with it."

"Aren't there pets on Neverwrong? Because if the answer is no, it will be the first thing that I fix." Tremble put a small plate of food down on the mat next to Choo Choo's water bowl. A rapidly wagging tail came as her thanks. "See that? See her tail wagging? She is communicating. She is expressing her appreciation for the little meal that I have placed in front of her. After she finishes eating and drinking a little water, she will probably lick my face with enthusiasm."

"There are pets on Neverwrong. Belladonna has a pet white panther named Houston. I just fail to understand the point. I fail to get the allure of the connection."

"You, then, my friend, have failed to have the right pet experience."

They all laughed as to prove their point; Choo Choo finished her meal, licked her face and jumped up on Laken's lap, planting kisses on his face.

"It was actually nice to be in the office for a little while. During the last couple of weeks, I have forgotten the value of normal."

"The medical community must be a constant challenge, Dana." Bridget cut up vegetables as Dana combined the ingredients for Alfredo sauce into a large bowl. Chicken and shrimp were the next ingredients for the noodle dish.

"It can be stressful, but also very rewarding. That must have been what drew Jasmine to healing in her world and medicine in ours."

"The stories about Jasmine's healing abilities are many and long. Even as a child, she was known to have a touch that could provide comfort as well as the complete relief from pain." Bridget finished her chopping duties and sat down at the counter. "Something that you might find interesting, Dana, is our world's belief regarding the process of healing. We believe that no matter the injury or illness, healing begins from the center. You first focus on the center of whatever is wrong. You meditate; you visualize the healing process, it becoming new again. True healing only occurs from the center out."

"One of our doctors has a similar philosophy. He is of Asian descent and trained at both Asian and American schools. He does an extensive amount of minor surgery and can make a patient scar-free, if they will follow his directions."

"You are speaking of Dr. Wu, aren't you?" Tremble smiled

as she said the name.

"I am indeed. Show them where your injury was."

"Oh, my, I had almost forgotten that." Bridget stood up as Tremble walked closer. "Come here, Laken, and look at Tremble's face."

Tremble smiled and moved her head from side to side for inspection.

"It is a very beautiful face." Laken looked like the words came out before he intended. His face began to turn red with embarrassment. "Ah, I meant—"

"You meant that Tremble is beautiful. This is not a secret, Laken. Look closely at the left side of her face, on her cheekbone. See anything?"

Tremble could feel his breath on her forehead as he stood over her and examined her face. It made Tremble uncomfortable.

"I don't see anything out of the ordinary."

"That's right, all because of Dr. Wu. I remember, Dana, he was amazing. We thought we were going to have to intercede with magic to fix Tremble's face."

"What happened?"

"Tremble was about seven years old?" Bridget's tone was questioning. Dana shook her head in a positive response. "She was at the home of her friend, VeVette. It was the little girl's birthday. Tremble got very excited, running after the family dog, a little cocker spaniel. She ran right through a sliding glass door. It was then that we discovered that Tremble's physical strength was increasing. A seven-year-old girl should not have been able to run through a glass door."

"See, it's another story involving a pet. No good comes from—"

"Shut up, Laken!" The three women said in unison, laughing at their timing.

"You are not going to win the argument about having pets." Tremble interjected. "I suggest you give that one up."

"Tremble had a huge deep cut down the side of her face." Dana set her cooking utensil down and appeared to be reliving the incident in her mind. "VeVette's mother had this beautiful cream carpet in her kitchen. It was popular then to have that low pile carpet in kitchens. I remember watching in slow motion as a pool of blood formed at Tremble's left foot, first on her white anklet, then in her patent leather white shoe and then on that carpet. I was in such shock, I could not move. It was VeVette's father, Brooks, who swept up Tremble, pressed a towel on her face, and headed for the car."

"I just love him. He has always been so good to me. I need to go visit."

"You will feel even more endeared to him when you hear the rest of this story. We got to the hospital and they got the bleeding stopped, but some intern wanted to sew you up. Your father was out of town at a medical convention. Brooks knew that Dr. Wu had a unique way of doing his surgery and healing process. Brooks went and retrieved him from the golf course so that he could do the stitching."

"That seems quite unusual even for the father of a close friend." Bridget tilted her head in a questioning manner as she commented.

"It was, in some respects. Most people do not know that Dr. Wu and Brooks served in the military together. They have a bond."

"So, get back to his procedure. What makes the way he does it so unusual?" Laken seemed interested. He kept looking at

Tremble's face.

"It is how he believes that healing should occur, from the inside, from the middle out. No matter the extent of the wound, his stitches are limited. It leaves the option for the healing to be open, not covered. The healing occurs from the inside out and it helps prevent pockets of infection from occurring." Dana ran her fingers down the side of Tremble's face. "It is why she does not have a scar. We went back every other day for two weeks. It was like magic."

"We would have stepped in, you know, and fixed it, if he hadn't—"

"That's precisely what makes it all the more beautiful. A natural magic made her beauty return. It was the magic of allowing this mishap to heal slowly and carefully. We should allow all our wounds to be cared for that way with patience and attention."

Laken again looked closely at the spot where Tremble's injury had once been. "I imagine that Queen Jasmine watched the work of this doctor from afar and approved of his methods."

"I think you are right, Laken." Dana went back to finishing the meal preparation. "I think that Jasmine could do very important work in this world."

A brightness came from behind the curtains in the living room, drawing them away from their conversation.

"Laken, please open the drapes. Belladonna is here. We need to speak with you and the others." It was CeCe beckoning them from behind the drapes.

Laken quickly pulled them open. The light was almost blinding. Belladonna and CeCe appeared to be outside in a very sunny courtyard. It reminded Tremble of the area where Jasmine and Forrest marry.

"It is high morning in our homeland." Bridget came out of

the kitchen area. She handed Dana a pair of what looked like sunglasses. "This shall help you with the brightness. It can be dangerous for mortal eyes to be exposed too long, even indirectly." Dana slipped the glasses on and turned back to face the window.

The light, while bright, did not bother Tremble. It did appear as though everything around Belladonna and CeCe was moving, including the interesting-looking man standing next to them.

"Greetings to all of you." Belladonna looked the most casual that Tremble had seen her. She wore a bejeweled and glamorous outfit, but it had the casualness of a jumpsuit. She looked like she might be appearing on an episode of *Charlie's Angels*. Tremble tried not to laugh. Belladonna stood in the middle with CeCe on one side and the man on the left. He looked very serious and very familiar.

"CeCe has given me an extensive rundown on this 'Suedama' person who has been stalking our girl. After an in-depth analysis of what we can pull of his genetic data, we do agree with the first conclusion that he is a Scordato clone. It seems to be a one cycle functioning clone. This means that it has one job and will self-destruct when that job is complete. Based on the scanty review of the last few months of Tremble's life, I think his purpose was to gather habit data. When the prophecy began its fulfillment, there was no longer need for it. I believe its life functions ended on the day that Jake came to see Tremble."

"What does that mean?"

"Tremble, in this case, all of the data that it had obtained by that point would go back to Scordato and 'Suedama' would be absorbed back into him." CeCe looked at the man to see if he would add anything, but he merely shook his head. "Now, there could have been another one created, but we see no evidence of that. From this point on, it will be hard for him to go unnoticed as there are so many watching you, at all times."

"So many? There are just a couple of you. We haven't seen any additional forces around." Dana adjusted the glasses.

"But, of course, you cannot detect them. That is the point." CeCe smiled and nodded. "There are at least six guardians assigned to Tremble during each twelve-hour shift. Most are invisible or disguised."

"Six!"

"Yes. That is not counting those who are with you at all times." Belladonna smiled and nodded at Bridget and Laken. "Surely, you must have suspected we would take every precaution to insure your safety. There has always been more guarding you than you could physically detect. You are a Royal, you must be guarded."

"I'm sorry, but this is ridiculous to me. Please move on to whatever else you need to tell us."

A stern look crossed Belladonna's face. CeCe and the man both looked uncomfortable. Belladonna cleared her throat.

"I understand that you now think you should go in search of your mother. That is not a wise course of action."

"Well, I'm afraid that I disagree with you. I think it is my only course of action. What else am I supposed to do? Life as I knew it is gone. My future is in this horrendous state of limbo because the fate of an entire kingdom seems to rest on my shoulders. I am surrounded by guardians who actually don't seem to have that great of a grasp of who is around me."

Bridget gasped. Dana gave Tremble an unhappy look. "Tremble, do you really think that is fair?"

"Mr. Suedama. He was hiding in plain sight."

"Tremble that is not a good example. Suedama was a clone

of Scordato, which was by its very creation hidden by great magic."

"All the more reason someone should have picked up on that. Listen, I am fine with it. No one needs to go to any extra trouble on my part. In a couple of weeks, I will legally be twenty-one. I am ready to fight my own battles. I want to find Jasmine and Forrest."

"Just how do you expect to do that, young lady?" Belladonna's disposition could change very quickly. "You have no training in tracking down such powerful beings as your parents. We have searched for them for years. What makes you think you will be able to find them?"

"I have no doubt that I can find them. The reason is very clear. They want me to find them. They want to see me. They will lead me to them, first one, and then the other."

"Tremble, you do not know what you are talking about." Belladonna now looked angry. "Laken, you will continue with Tremble's training until we send for her."

"NO! He will continue Tremble's training until Tremble is ready to go find Jasmine. Then, he will accompany Tremble because obviously she does not know how to navigate travel between worlds. Now, I will lower my voice and stop referring to myself in the third person."

"I forbid it." Belladonna's voice was strong and clear. A chair appeared behind her and she sat down.

"That's funny." Tremble rolled her eyes.

"Funny? I don't see what you think is funny."

"Mom, tell Belladonna what happens when you forbid me to do something."

"Really, Tremble, I think you should stop this conversation. We can talk about this later."

"Tell her. She needs to understand."

"Go ahead, Dana. I am listening. What does our darling Tremble do when forbidden to do something? Does she stomp her feet? Does she cry?" Belladonna's tone was mocking.

"No, none of that. She was raised to have better behavior." Dana's tone matched Belladonna's. "Telling her that she cannot do something turns on a power within her that insures she will accomplish that task with great accuracy, even if it is dangerous. She gets the power from Jasmine. She gets the tenacity from me. Do not forbid her to do anything, Belladonna. You don't have the power to stop her."

Chapter Four

THE GAUNTLET HAD come down. The conversation with Belladonna ended with Dana's warning words. Tremble saw a troubled look cross CeCe's face as Belladonna rose and walked away before the screen went black.

"You should not cross Her Royal Highness." Laken looked Tremble squarely in the eyes. "She has made great sacrifices for you and Queen Jasmine."

"I appreciate that, Laken. No one seems to understand though that this is *my* life. I need to make my own choices, even regarding this outlandish situation. I will not be a puppet with others pulling my strings. I will walk into my own destiny."

"Very well, Tremble." Dana and Tremble gasped as they turned and saw that CeCe was in the room behind them.

"How did you—?" Tremble's mind began racing as she thought about the power that CeCe must possess.

"I can travel quickly when the need arises. All protectors can. You have underestimated our powers." CeCe looked from Tremble to Dana. "I want you both to tell me why you think that Jasmine is summoning Tremble. I have a feeling that Dana knows something about this process as well."

They sat down in the living room before Dana began.

"After Tremble was born, there were a few moments that Jasmine and I had together, alone. She did not tell me not to share what she said with Andrew, I just decided to keep the information to myself. The main thing she said was that while she was suppressing most of Tremble's powers, she was going to give Tremble the power to summon her. I remember her clearly saying that Tremble would always have the power to call out to her. Jasmine wanted Tremble to be able to summon her biological mother; her magical mother was what she said. Tremble's instincts would tell her if the need arose."

"Did she specifically mention that she might visit Tremble in her dreams?" CeCe's tone was still serious and stern.

"Yes, Jasmine said that as Tremble got older she might try to visit her to begin to prepare her to learn who she was."

"Tremble, do you ever remember seeing Jasmine in your dreams before you knew about her?" Bridget joined the conversation.

"I don't think so. Despite the fact that I would not have recognized her, I think I would have remembered her because she is so beautiful. I cannot explain it. From the first time I saw an image of her, I felt a connection on some level. It was like I recognized her somehow."

"It is logical. It is natural." CeCe paused for a moment. "Tell me about this dream."

"Jasmine is in a forest. First, she is deep within it and almost completely hidden by trees. With each successive dream, she seems to be closer." Tremble stopped and thought. "Actually, I think I am the one who gets closer. She is still in the woods. It is very dark around her. I really had not realized that until just now. I think that is why I feel so strongly about finding her. I get closer to her. I find her."

"It is a very dangerous thing for you to try to do." CeCe's words were direct. She raised her hand before Tremble could speak. "I am not going to try to stop you. I told Belladonna the same. I am just saying that it is dangerous even if Jasmine is willing you to do it."

"CeCe, you agreed to this idea? You told Belladonna that?" The look on Laken's face was one of disbelief. "How did she respond?"

"Her words exactly were 'let it be.' She might challenge the decisions of her niece. She will not challenge Jasmine." CeCe's statement silenced Laken.

"Then, what are Belladonna's instructions?" Bridget changed the direction of the conversation.

"She wants us to prepare Tremble as best as we can. It would be helpful if we had the time between now and Tremble's twenty-first birthday to allow her to test her power. Belladonna does ask that we try to convince Tremble not to try to leave until her birthday has passed."

"I am not unreasonable. I want to learn as much as I possibly can. I am determined to carry this out. I hope that Jasmine will continue to visit me in my dreams. Perhaps, she will help me better understand what I should do."

"Tremble, I feel this with all my heart." Dana sat down next to her daughter. "You must call out to Jasmine and ask her what to do. I know that she will answer you, if she can."

"Dana is right." CeCe's expression softened. "I have no doubt that Jasmine will if she has the ability to do so."

"Meaning?"

"Meaning, if she is not hindered in some way. We do not know where she is. We do not know where Forrest is. They may be close; they may be far. They may be captive or free." CeCe turned and made eye contact with Bridget before she continued. "We need to take your training to a new level. We need to sharpen our focus." CeCe took a deep breath. "Bridget and I are planning to go into the office tomorrow. We have decided that our decision to disband the company was a hasty one. We have made the excuse that we have been gone on business and a few days of vacation. We are going to empower several on our team to be in charge for the next few months and tell them that Bridget and I have decided to tour Europe. Tremble, you have been out due to some sudden surgery your mother needed to have."

"I hope my illness wasn't serious." Dana chuckled and winked.

"Serious enough that you needed your daughter's help, but you are on the road to a full recovery."

"Glad to hear it."

"Your internship is almost halfway complete." Bridget began to speak as Dana began to walk into the kitchen. "Everyone at the agency knows that you were doing an excellent job. We have decided that you are going to work from home on an extensive research project. This will also allow you to continue to help your mother."

"That's an interesting idea, but wouldn't I be reporting to someone at the office as I have been?"

"No, I will make sure that our supervisory team understands that you will be reporting to me via email and Skype." CeCe looked very serious. "I will tell them that this research is regarding our competitors. No one will question my motives."

"Tremble, no one questions CeCe. You have been around long enough to know that."

"Do I need to go into the office with you tomorrow?"

"No. You will be taking a trip though." CeCe turned to Laken. "Belladonna wishes for Tremble to attempt a visit to the Library."

"What?" Laken's eyes grew big.

"You heard me. Belladonna thinks it will be a good test of her current powers."

"CeCe, you don't really think she has the ability—" Bridget's comment was cut short.

"It is hard for me to imagine that Tremble currently has the ability to do this. Nevertheless, Bridget, you know that Belladonna has the capacity to understand Tremble in a way we cannot. She can gauge her abilities better than either of us can."

"I don't understand." Tremble put her head in her hands. "Isn't the Library in Neverwrong? How can Belladonna know what I can do better than you?"

"I will take that first question, CeCe." Bridget made an image appear before them. It was the interior of the Library they had seen when Tremble was first shown Scordato and The Seven. "The Royal Family of Neverwrong, your family, has many powers. Some of these are unique to them, meaning that other magical beings do not possess them. One of these is the ability to teleport to other locations in their minds."

"Teleport? What?"

As Tremble asked the question, Dana appeared at the edge of the dining room with a bowl of salad in her hand. She set the bowl down and joined them in the living room.

"May I?" Laken walked over to where Bridget was standing.

"Certainly, I forgot that you might possess this ability."

"Not to the extent that Tremble should be able to, but I will have the ability to accompany her." Laken paused and looked first at Tremble, then at Dana to see if they understood. "Half of my genetic makeup came from the Royal family."

"We know that." A smile began to form on Tremble's face. "I've been thinking about calling you Cuz."

"I don't understand."

"Oh, Laken, it would be so much easier if you had grown up here with me. Cuz is short for cousin, as in a relative."

"Oh, I see. Cousins are the children of your parents' siblings. Is that correct?" Everyone nodded affirmatively. "Do I have any cousins, CeCe?"

"Well, none that I know of on your father's side of the family. However, we do not know about your Royal genetics, so it is hard to tell. Tremble is not exactly wrong with her joking remark. You are cousins, albeit distant ones."

"So, if I learn how to do this mind teleport thing, Laken will be able to go with me. That is reassuring. I really wouldn't want to go alone."

"You shall learn. There is no doubt. I shall be honored to accompany you, if I have enough of the Royal DNA in me to allow it. I do believe that I can adequately describe the process as Belladonna took me on a short excursion within Neverwrong. It could be compared to what humans now call virtual reality. You can journey to another location, even another realm. You do it in your mind. Your brain makes the journey. While humans have worked on creating a simulated environment to travel to, these journeys are real, in a physical sense."

"Okay, that is a good comparison, I guess. I get an idea of

what you mean. I don't understand what you meant when you said, 'real, in a physical sense.'"

"With virtual reality, you are usually entering an environment that has been created for that purpose. It might be a simulation of a real place. With mind teleporting, your brain travels to the real location and you will be able to interact with the environment."

Tremble still had a look of confusion on her face. Bridget made the screen come to life with a different view.

"Let me help you now by showing you that is very special to me."

The image before them sprung to life. It was incredibly beautiful.

"Oh my, look at all the animals."

Dana smiled as she pointed and looked to see if Tremble was watching. It reminded Tremble of the many times her parents had taken her to visit some new location. Her mother always had a wide-eyed look of pure wonder and enjoyment as she discovered something new.

"This is the Land of Sojourn. It is the domain of the animals of Neverwrong. As was shared earlier, we do have pets in a similar manner to this world. They are not owned in the same sense. Animals choose to come and spend time with you. It may be hours, days, or weeks. Eventually, they will go back to Sojourn. Only in cases of extreme emergency, or to provide care for these animals, would a citizen of Neverwrong go there. This is how we visit. We view the animals. I can summon one of my old friends."

Bridget closed her eyes and began to whisper. Tremble could not make out the words. A few moments passed and a beautiful giraffe came walking out of a wooded area. It came right up to where Bridget was standing.

"That giraffe is green." Dana made her pronouncement and it broke Tremble's concentration.

"I hadn't noticed that. Bridget, this giraffe is a friend of yours?"

"Yes, she certainly is. Her name is Miranda. I raised her."

"How does she know that you are here? Can she see you?"

"We are not certain about that." CeCe joined the conversation and walked toward the screen. Miranda walked over to the side of the screen where CeCe was standing. "But, as you just observed, we know that the animals of Neverwrong have the power to sense when a being they are connected to is either near or is summoning them. We think that once a summons has begun, the animal can hear our voices. Miranda would recognize mine as well as Bridget's."

"So, if I walk up and stand between you two, what will happen?"

"Let's find out."

Tremble walked up and stood between Bridget and CeCe. This put her about in the middle of the screen. Nothing happened. Miranda did not move.

"Say her name."

"Miranda." Tremble watched closely, but the giraffe did not move.

"Miranda, I must introduce you to my new friend, Tremble." Miranda walked back over to where Bridget stood. "Now, speak to her."

"Hello, Miranda." Still nothing happened.

"It must be that there needs to have been a physical introduction. We just do not know how animal powers work."

"There went my career as a giraffe whisperer." Everyone looked at Tremble and smirked. "Okay, enough of the humor.

Continue explaining how this relates to teleporting."

"Yes, if you had teleported into this location, you would be able to pet Miranda. You could feel the sensation and so would she, but you would not physically be there."

"Excuse me for saying so, Bridget, but that just sounds strange." Dana scrunched her eyes and tilted her head. She seemed to be trying to process what Bridget said.

"I'm sure it does. It is how our magical world works. Like some things in the mortal world, there is no explanation, it just is."

"I heard a bell, Dana. Does that mean dinner is ready?" Laken smiled in anticipation.

"Oh, my, yes. I forgot." Dana jumped up and ran toward the kitchen. "I hope the bread isn't burnt."

"Well, we haven't heard the smoke alarm. That's a good sign." Laken said in a low voice once Dana had left the room.

Bridget shook her head at Laken's attempt at humor as she blew a kiss to Miranda right before she made the screen disappear. They headed toward the dining room as Dana came out of the kitchen with a platter of food.

"I heard that, Laken."

"How could you have possibly?" He looked a little uncomfortable about Dana's quick comeback.

"I'm a mother, Laken. I can hear everything."

They settled into dinner, as everyone seemed ravenous. Tremble used the silence to think further about the concept of teleporting. As she looked around the table, each person seemed deep in thought.

"Belladonna wants me to visit the Library." Tremble broke the silence. "Why there?"

"There is vast knowledge within the Library." CeCe set her

fork down and sipped her drink before she continued. "As you know, the Library is where Amadeus was left and the location where he became Scordato. However, it is much more than that. The Seven were very young when they left the mountain. However, all of them tell the same story. When they were still together with their parents, the Library was central to their family. Apparently, there are many more rooms—a mansion probably—within the mountain. It is the Library where the majority of their time was spent and where the children learned from their parents about magic."

"Many of the Royals, including your parents, have visited the Library through teleportation." Bridget picked up the conversation. "Some have spent large periods of time through the years attempting to read all of the volumes in the vast collection. There are ancient books from all civilizations as well as from many different worlds—magic and non-magical. A few of the volumes are off-limits to the Royals."

"That is one thing that Belladonna is very curious about." Laken interrupted. "She wonders if you might be able to access these forbidden books."

"What do you mean?"

"Through teleporting, you will be able to go and walk around the Library, in a virtual sense. You will be able to select a book off the shelf and read it. The sisters, and their descendants, of The Seven, have been more successful in viewing some of the ancient books about spells and potions. Baldric and his descendants can most easily access the volumes that deal with military maneuvers or histories of wars in different kingdoms. There is a selection of books cannot be chosen by either group. Those have an enchantment protecting them."

Laken paused and took a drink of the tall glass of water in

front of him. Tremble noticed that, for a second, she could see the water travelling down his throat. She closed her eyes and shook her head.

"What's wrong, Tremble?" Bridget seemed to notice Tremble's action.

"Oh, nothing. It's all a lot to process."

Bridget gave her a questioning look but did not press further.

"Belladonna thinks that since you are the first to descend from both King Baldric and Queen Perpetua, you may be able to overcome the enchantment that has protected those books."

"What about Scordato? Didn't he say that he had read every book in the Library?"

"That's a good point, Tremble." CeCe leaned back in her chair. "We feel that Scordato probably has created these enchantments. Possibly based on some of the knowledge he gained from the most ancient magical books. We think that he allowed his sisters to have access to those with knowledge of spells and potions so that their knowledge might grow and their powers increase. It is obvious that he loved his sisters, no matter what happened between them."

"Then why would he allow Baldric and his descendants the ability to read anything within the Library? Scordato does not appear to have any kind feeling toward his brother."

"The true answer to that question is not known. The Royal Sisters speculated that he wished to empower Baldric and those after him to be able to protect the other lines of the family."

"Yes, what CeCe says is true." Laken took another helping of the pasta entrée. "Belladonna says that she remembers her mother and grandmother speculating that Scordato wished to insure that his sisters and their families were protected from encroaching kingdoms, near and far."

"That still doesn't explain why I might be able to access the forbidden books."

"We are hoping that perhaps Scordato does not have a dual spell on them. He may have one spell to prevent access to the sisters' line and another spell for Baldric's line. We hope he has set them up that way."

"Because?"

"Because, in your case, they would cancel each other out. If someone from both lines tried to access it, the spell might be confused. A dual spell should be the only thing that could prevent you."

"What makes you think that Scordato didn't think of that?"

"It's all speculation. We know though that he was young with less experience when he developed these levels of protection. The Seven began returning to the Library via teleporting soon after that initial encounter with their brother. All of them were still in their youth then."

"How did this Library come to be? For that matter, how did my ancestors come to live inside that mountain?"

"That is a wonderful reason for us to give you a deeper history lesson, my dear." Bridget rose from her spot at the table. "It is one that Dana will also be interested in hearing. For that reason, I am going to do something you shall rarely see me do." Bridget paused. She looked around the room. No one said a word. "Since no one seems to be asking, I will tell you what that is. I am going to clean up the dining room and kitchen using magic." Again, silence. "Why is no one saying anything?"

CeCe started to speak, but Dana beat her to it. "I have been waiting for several weeks for you to say that. What has been stopping you?"

Everyone roared with laughter, including Bridget. She began

to chant. "Dinner, dinner, everything we wished. Now be gone, every single dish." Her arms rose with the movements of an orchestra conductor. By the time, she put them back down, every dish had disappeared and both rooms were clean.

"You've really got to teach me how to do that." Dana's tone was serious as she looked around both rooms before following the rest of the group out onto the back deck.

For a few moments, they watched the beautiful sunset that was putting on a show in between a cluster of trees at the edge of the Dawson's backyard. There was something about the shimmering light as it danced through the tall bark that summoned Tremble. It mesmerized her. Laken broke the silence.

"I have a series of Royal memories that Her Royal Highness has given me the ability to share. I'm sure that you may be tired of watching these glimpses into the past, but it is the best way to accurately relay this information to you."

"Oh, I do not mind the Neverwrong movies and I think Mom loves them." Tremble turned to Dana who shook her head.

"If we hadn't just eaten, I would make some popcorn."

"Very well then, with CeCe's and Bridget's permission, I will begin."

The two women nodded as Laken made the largest screen Tremble had yet seen appear in her backyard. Dana leaned over to her.

"Your father would have loved this."

"Wouldn't he though? But, like all the technology in the house, he wouldn't have been able to figure out how it worked." Tremble and her mother exchanged an understanding smile.

"The first image I am going to present is from the memory of Queen Perpetua."

"Laken, I'm sorry to interrupt." Dana had her hand raised,

like a student in a class, as she began to speak. "How are you able to get a memory from Queen Perpetua?"

"Excellent question. This is something that Tremble needs to learn because she might have reason to do it, at some point. As we have told you previously, The Seven are all now physically dead. The curse that Scordato put on them allowed for their immortality to only be in mental form. Of course, this is like being in a prison. They are confined to portraits. Comparatively speaking, you could liken them to paintings in a museum. First, it was thought this would also confine their magical abilities and it certainly does to an extent. Yet, they do still have the ability to move within their frame, so to speak. They can also still perform spells. It was actually Gwenora who discovered this."

A portrait appeared on the screen. The woman was very beautiful. She seemed to be much younger than Tremble expected.

"Is this Gwenora? She looks quite young."

"Yes, it is a sad story." Bridget began to answer. "An enchantress is not immune to the problems that sometimes occur to female beings as they attempt to give birth to a child. Gwenora experienced severe complications while delivering her second child, a son. Queen Perpetua was the healer of the family, like Jasmine. She was in a neighboring land healing Baldric after those who were attacking our neighbor kingdom impaled him. Perpetua could not be summoned in time to help Gwenora. She was only in her late twenties. She was the first to experience the judgment of Scordato's curse."

"Oh, how horrible!" Dana verbalized what Tremble was feeling.

"Yes, Perpetua never forgave herself. It only deepened her anger toward both of her brothers."

"Belladonna favors her."

"She does indeed, Tremble. I know from my experience growing up near Her Royal Highness that she spent a lot of time in the Hall of Royals visiting with Gwenora."

"All of these portraits are in one place?"

"Yes, at first, they were kept at their individual family estates. By the time all of the siblings had finally reached this state, their children and even their grandchildren were grown. It was decided that they should be reunited. Partially because they knew that eventually this time would come and it might be beneficial for them to be together."

"Show Tremble the room." CeCe pointed to the screen.

"Very well."

The view changed to a circular room. Occupying the wall space were huge portraits that appeared to be life size. The view changed and Tremble was able to see the room from the top looking down. The middle of the room had a garden-like appearance. As she was watching it, the view changed to show an image of the courtyard where Jasmine and Forrest were married. It changed once more to a view of the Land of Sojourn that Bridget had shown them earlier.

"It's like their own television of sorts. They can choose different views. It was developed by one of Baldric's grandsons who is very astute in magical technology."

"Magical technology. I don't even want to know." Tremble shook her head and chuckled. "Are they in a circle so that they can see each other and communicate?"

"Yes, that is correct. It is also possible for each of the portraits to be pulled back into its own room."

Laken showed an image of one of the portraits moving in reverse back into the wall. The next view showed it turning around into a larger room with a sitting area. Several people entered, sat down, and began talking to the portrait.

"Visiting hours, I presume." Dana spoke, never taking her eyes off the screen.

"Exactly. It gives the family privacy."

With a wave of his hand, Laken made the image disappear and in its place was a panoramic view of the Library. Tremble quickly counted four of the sisters there including two that she now recognized as Perpetua and Gwenora. Both of them were still in their physical states, in their youth.

"This is a good example of how the Library has been used by this first generation and those who have come afterward. You can see that Gwenora is summoning a book from one of the high shelves."

They watched as Gwenora's lips moved while she motioned for the book to come toward her. Gwenora returned to her seat and began to read. On the other side of the large room, another sister sat on a bench within the wall. Using her finger, she pointed at several of the books as she whispered a spell. None of them moved.

"That is Verina over there." CeCe pointed to the left side of the screen. "I've always thought she was an interesting one. She is the baby of the family and was frightfully independent. She is the only one in the family who dared to marry a mortal. The girl had spunk."

"Married a mortal?" Tremble let out an infectious laugh.

"Yes, her husband was from this world. His tragic young death was a shock to the public. She travelled into the future to convince him to come to Neverwrong."

"To the future? My goodness. She was a time traveler?"

Tremble stopped laughing and rose to get a better look at

Verina. The young woman seemed to be chattering forcefully with Perpetua as she repeatedly pointed back to the bookcase.

"Yes, she was." CeCe joined Tremble on the left side of the screen. "I spent some time with Verina when I was in the early years of my training with the Bureau. Well, I guess I should correctly say that I spent some time with her portrait. She told me that she learned about time travel in one of those very volumes you see there. As a teenager in this world might rebel by staying out too late or dating someone her parents did not approve of, Verina decided to travel. Her trips were numerous and into various eras in the human world. Her favorite was the twentieth century and it was there that she found the man of her dreams. You will not find a photograph of him anywhere. He would not allow it. Being a mortal, he lived out his natural life—no more, no less. His identity was kept under the utmost secrecy. Obviously, the general citizens of Neverwrong, of the time, could not have possibly known who he was. I only now know because I was privy to the classified information held within the files of the Bureau." CeCe grew silent. She took a drink from a tray that Bridget had brought outside while she was talking.

"Oh, come on, CeCe, you're going to tell us, right? You've got to tell us."

"No, I am not. It would be a compromise of my duties. But, I will say this. He was a rebel of his time. That is where the attraction began. He was a rebel, just like Verina."

"That describes a lot of famous people who died young in the twentieth century." Dana took the drink that Bridget offered her. "I presume that this is another faked celebrity death."

"It makes you wonder about a lot of people, doesn't it, Mom?"

"Yes, and this is another thing your father would just love."

IT BEGAN TO RAIN, so the group moved inside. Before continuing the conversation, it was decided that they would change into their nightclothes and move into a rarely used room of the Dawson house.

Much like his office, the den was truly Andrew's sanctuary. It was full of technology as well as a vast collection of movies and music. Since Tremble had gone off to college, Dana did not use the room much. She preferred to curl up with a book in her bedroom or watch a movie in the living room. Tremble had discovered this when she would return home on break and find that the den was covered in a layer of dust. The person who liked everything spotless was not entering the room at all. It surprised Tremble that her mother had suggested they spend the rest of the evening there.

"Wow! This room is incredible." Laken's wide eyes matched the Spiderman lounge pants he was wearing.

"You would have made an excellent teenage boy." Tremble let her mouth say what her mind was thinking.

"I was a teenage boy. You are laughing at the pants. I saw them advertised in one of those colorful paper things that come within the newspaper. The models looked casual and cool. I thought it was popular attire." Laken looked at CeCe and Bridget. They were trying very hard not to laugh.

"It would be cool if you were eleven, early twenties, not so much. We will not allow it to affect our view of what you have to say." Tremble's fake serious tone only slightly helped her conceal her amusement.

Laken pulled off the matching T-shirt he was wearing and

replaced it with a navy sweatshirt that magically appeared in his hand. The action about caused Tremble to gasp as she saw the abs that had been hiding underneath. Laken was not eleven. Making eye contact with him, Tremble realized that he had seen her response. She looked away as he slightly smiled.

"We shall resume where we probably should have started, with what we know about the beginnings of the family who became the Royals of Neverwrong."

This time, instead of a screen, the whole room changed. Tremble heard her mother gasp as they looked around. Instantly, they were in the most beautiful room Tremble had ever seen. The wall covering was a rich royal blue from the ceiling to the chair rail. There were thin lines of gold within its texture. As Tremble looked closer, she realized that the lines would change and move, creating vertical and horizontal lines, then change again to diagonal or circular ones. It made the room look like it was constantly moving. The blue color also changed to burgundy and then emerald green before again reverting to blue. The change did not occur all at once, but in waves of color, reinforcing the feeling of movement. The chair rail and wainscot was a rich gold and glimmered like a shiny coin. Images of exotic animals appeared on the wainscot. It gave the allusion that the lions and tigers were walking around the edge of the room. Tremble was mesmerized until her peripheral vision caught sight of a large bird swooping across the ceiling. Behind it was a yellow sky with lavender clouds drifting by. She paused on the image as her mind adjusted to the colors of this other world. As she took in the surroundings, it occurred to her that they were not in the Library. This room, while similar in nature and use, looked very different from where they had seen Scordato. She imagined that the room must be in a mansion in Neverwrong.

Her gaze broke as she heard the clack-clack-clack of someone's shoes on the floor. The sound made her realize that a smooth marble covered the area below her feet. At different locations across the vast floor, Tremble could also see beautiful carpets. They looked so soft that she felt drawn to reach down and touch them. As she did so, she drew her hand back quickly; shocked that she could indeed feel the luxurious softness.

"How can I possibly feel that?" Tremble rose and looked around the room, searching to see one of her group. Laken walked into her view.

"It would appear that Belladonna is right. You do have the power to teleport and become part of where you go."

"It's really amazing." Bridget appeared from behind a tall ornate chair. "It appears that she can teleport to the past as well."

"Time travelling teleporting. Her Royal Highness will be most impressed."

"Okay, you two, enough. Do I need to be concerned about any of this? Any rules of teleporting that I need to know?"

Tremble watched as CeCe came into view. The three of them looked at each other very seriously before CeCe spoke.

"Do not try to occupy the same space as someone else."

"What?" Tremble's face took on a pinched and confused look.

"Do not try to stand in the same space as someone else, even accidentally. Back away from wherever the person is headed in his or her movements."

"Why?" As the question left her lips, a cold chill passed over Tremble. Her mind zoomed back to the first time she was shown such a view from the past. She had not realized then that she was really within the image. She had teleported. A frail Scordato in rags had passed right through her. She had felt it. "Why?" She cautiously asked again.

"Because two souls cannot occupy the same space. It could have serious consequences for either one or both."

Tremble looked CeCe in the eyes. "Serious consequences?"

"Possession, or worse."

"Worse?"

"Worse, as in you do not want to know."

Tremble turned and found that her mother had found a place to sit in the corner, near a bookcase. None of the ancestor family was anywhere close to the location. She saw that Dana had a look of worry. Tremble gave her a quick smile and changed the subject.

"Okay. We are here to learn about the family history, correct?"

"Yes. Everyone get comfortable." Laken looked around the room. "There are no better ones to tell you the history than this first generation of Royals. Much of this is in Queen Perpetua's letters. Hearing her and her sisters talk about their parents is a wonderful way for you to begin to learn about who you really are."

They all became silent. Tremble began to relax her mind and try to listen. She glanced in the direction of her mother and found that Bridget was beside her. Her mother's head was tilted to one side. She seemed to be concentrating. Tremble allowed her gaze to drift back to the room around her. Soft female voices grew louder as the story began.

"Tell us, sister. Help us remember our life before we came here."

Tremble thought that the young voice was that of Verina, the future time traveler.

"Only a smidgen, my little one." Perpetua's response was

gentle. "My dear, must you always sit on the floor? We have such lovely chairs."

"Oh, Pet, you know I do despise to be all confined in proper seating. It is bad enough that I must be in this frilly dress. I do so long to dress like the boys do."

Verina sat on the floor in front of a vast fireplace. So large it was that it seemed to take up an entire wall. The young girl had a deep navy dress on with many layers. Tremble was surprised to see that the fabric resembled corduroy as she thought of that as a more modern style of fabric.

"Tell me what you remember about arriving here. I do so love this story. Our time in the mountain is just a blur to me, a speck of memory."

"Me, too." A small blur in yellow ran into Tremble's view. It was a very young Gwenora. Her small size and quick scamper made her appear like a little bird floating around the room.

"You two were just toddling around when we made our way down the mountain." Perpetua paused, deep in thought for a moment before her gaze returned to the anxious faces before her. "I suppose since both of you have been so good this afternoon, I shall tell you the story." Perpetua reached out with both arms to the girls and they sat down within her embrace. "Why don't I just start at the very beginning of our family story? Well, I suppose I should say the very beginning that I remember, even before our home in the mountain."

The two girls looked at each other with eyes of amazed curiosity as they quickly nodded and looked back at their older sister.

"When our brothers and I were just little tykes barely able to wobble around on two feet, I remember the house that we lived in then. Abelia and Crispina were just babies then and the rest of you were still glimmers in our father's eyes."

The two giggled and Tremble could see that they were glowing with delight. She did not see one distinct color to each of their auras, but more a blending of many. A look of solemnness quickly followed as Gwenora spoke.

"I do so wish I remembered Amadeus. How sad for us to not have our other brother."

These words told Tremble that the scene they were viewing occurred before the family returned to the mountain, before they met Scordato and learned of the curse he had put on all of them. Perpetua was silent for a moment before she continued.

"We lived in a very old house, as I remember. It was dark and scary with a huge circular staircase in the very middle that rose up four stories high to a small attic. It would take the three of us quite a while to climb up there each morning. Our little legs had to work hard to carry us from one large step to the next. We would make the climb each day though, as the attic was our most very favorite place. It was a land of wonder to us."

"Why?" Both of the younger sisters asked.

"Much like this beautiful room in which we now sit, the room was filled with treasures. There was chest after chest filled with costumes and jewels. The brothers and I created a multitude of adventures, and we honed our magical skills as we imagined worlds far away."

"Where was this place? Where was this house?" Verina eyes grew big with wonder.

Perpetua was silent. She reached down to them and pulled her sisters close. "I do not know. I only remember small passages of time. Our mother and father only spoke of it later in sadness. I think we left there by force, not by choice."

"I barely remember them, Pet." Verina fought back tears.

"I only remember how our mother smelled. I remember roses, soft and lingering." Gwenora made no pretense. She allowed the tears to flow.

"I remember the day we came to this mountain. With one hand, father held mine. With the other, he grasped a large basket that held both Abelia and Crispina. He was very strong. Our mother held the hands of our brothers. It was nothing but a mountain when we arrived. I watched with eyes of wonder as my father fashioned our entire world within that mountain with his magic. It was a huge house with many rooms, but the centermost room was our beloved Library."

Perpetua paused for a moment and Tremble took that time to glance at Laken. Instead of watching the view before them, he was intently watching her. The fact that she now had noticed him doing so did not dissuade him from concentrating on her. As their eyes met, Tremble could hear his voice, his thoughts. An awareness of that seemed to pass through his eyes, and he quickly broke his gaze. Perpetua resumed talking.

"Our father was the Supreme Enchanter Marcellus. His powers were vast and unsurpassed. He chose for his wife, an enchantress to match his skill. Her Royal Highness Claudia was the most powerful enchantress that her kingdom had ever known. Legends have been built on the works of their hands."

"Why did they come to the mountain? Why did they not take their family to a grand palace somewhere with lots of people around? It seems strange for such powerful ones to seclude themselves."

Verina rose from her sister's arms and began walking around. Tremble noticed that one of the young girl's boots was coming unlaced.

"Father told us that there was a great evil that would come upon us. Our only hope was to hide ourselves and hope that it did not find us."

"How did we come to be enchanters? Are there others like us?" Gwenora squirmed out of Perpetua's embrace and joined her sister as she wandered around the room.

"Your minds are full of questions today. I shall not be able to quench your desires with all of the answers."

Perpetua laughed and Tremble saw a youthful beauty. Yet, she also noticed that there was an undertone of worry, of anticipating.

"Our magic is a gift. We must use it with kindness and compassion. Our mother told the story of when she was a little girl when there was a sickness that came upon the people of her land. Many, old and young, began to die. Her heart was sad, as her closest companion had also taken ill. Our mother knew little of her magic, but in a dream it came to her that she could heal her friend. As she awoke, the words to a spell were on her lips. The words were true. Her friend lived as well as many others. The sickness left the land. Claudia became a healer."

"You are a healer, isn't that right?"

"I try to be. I will teach our healing spells to you one day."

"Why couldn't our parents' powers protect them?" Gwenora looked at her oldest sister with big, sad eyes.

"The evil that took our parents swept in like a thief in the night. They may have not known what took them."

"Took them?" Verina gave Perpetua a questioning look.

"Yes, our parents were taken."

"Then, how do we know they are dead?"

"It is not something that I want to tell you."

"Why not?"

Tremble had forgotten that a fourth sister was in the room. From a distant corner, a very tall young woman came. Her height was a good four inches taller than Perpetua. Her hair was long and straight, and a beautiful strawberry red. Despite the flowing gown, the look reminded Tremble of how young women appeared in the 1970s. It was as if this girl was from another time. Tremble was shocked as she heard a melodious voice. The girl sounded as if she were almost singing the words.

"You should not hold back, my sister. We do not protect them when it is on guard they need to be."

Perpetua gave the sister who had spoken a long and serious look. Tremble could see that Perpetua was carefully pondering what she had just heard, weighing the decision that would be her response.

"Perhaps, my wise sister, you are right. Dear Abelia, you remind me of the words of our father. My dear, you are so like him. We are blessed to have his wisdom through you."

Abelia. Tremble's mind raced thinking about the order of birth for the sister. It amazed her that instantly before her eyes appeared a list of them with name and portrait. The names were Perpetua, Abelia, Crispina, Gwenora, Elsavetta, and Verina. The unusualness of their names matched the individuality of their beauty. Abelia was the second oldest sister.

"Our powers must have a keen awareness of our adversaries. Baldric is not the only warrior in this family. We must all be warriors."

Nodding in agreement, Perpetua returned her gaze to her younger sisters. "This would only be the mist of a memory to our youngest siblings. We were all together in the mountain for several years. Baldric and I were still young ourselves." Perpetua hesitated. Tremble wondered if the woman was thinking of Amadeus. "We knew that we were hiding from something, someone. Our father did not allow us to play outside in the real world, only in the one he created."

"Created? I do not understand." Verina looked from sister to sister for understanding.

"As I have said, our father had amazing powers. Yet, he was not frivolous with the use of them. He did make indulgences, however, when it came to his children. He greatly enjoyed seeing us at play, but he would not allow us to venture outside of our mountain home. There were dangers lurking there, he said. He created an outside for us. It was always delightful, unusual, and adventurous."

"Gather the other sisters, Verina." Abelia interrupted Perpetua's speech. "Bring them to us so that they can hear Perpetua." Abelia turned to Perpetua. Tremble could see that her expression was intense for a young woman of her age. "It is time to tell them why we left the mountain. It is time they know why we are in Neverwrong."

Chapter
Five

"THIS MEMORY, what Perpetua is about to tell her sisters, have you heard this story?"

As Abelia had instructed her youngest sister to gather the others, Laken had paused the view they were seeing and asked if they wanted to take a break.

"Actually, I have not."

Laken began some stretching movements. CeCe, Bridget, and Dana had left the room when he had paused the view. Tremble and Laken had a few minutes alone.

"My training included many aspects of the history of the Royal Family. Most of it focused on their lives in Neverwrong or trying to learn more about Scordato. I have peripheral knowledge of Marcellus and Claudia, but only as they relate to their children."

"All of this is beyond my comprehension. Yet, it is familiar in some way, like a story I read in a book long ago."

Laken had restored the room to its original look while they were taking a break. Tremble walked around and absentmindedly fingered items that remained on the shelves of her father's bookcase. Her index finger traced the outline of a Popsicle stick picture frame she had made in the first grade. The sticks were painted bright yellow and there were ancient pieces of macaroni decorating it. Within the frame was Tremble's smiling face, a front tooth missing, hugging the family's first pet. The white ball of fur reminded Andrew of the small balls of soft fiber that he kept in a jar in his medical office. It was Dana who gave the long-haired white Persian cat its name—Cotton. The memory made her smile. She set the frame back down as she turned toward Laken. The memory slipped away as the reality of what they were about to view returned.

"I haven't even heard what will be said, but my mind immediately wonders if there could be a connection between what happened to Perpetua's parents and Scordato."

"Your wisdom and understanding is growing." CeCe's words made them turn in her direction. "This is the type of logical thought that shall help you not only find Jasmine and Forrest but will also help you determine the best way to combat Scordato."

"We have hoped that your powers would not be limited to just magic." Bridget came through the doorway with Dana behind her. They were carrying trays of beverages and snacks. "I am so glad that the most common of your senses is firmly intact."

"I do not understand what you just said, Bridget." The look of confusion that crossed Laken's face was almost humorous to Tremble. "Tremble is perfect. How could you think otherwise?"

Tremble could not look at her mother, CeCe, or Bridget. She knew that what was passing between them would put her over the edge between laughter and embarrassment. The fact that Laken had been groomed to adore her was not a comfortable secret. Bridget was the one who got them past the moment.

"Laken, I should have been clearer. I meant that I was pleased that besides her obvious magical powers, Tremble has also learned a good deal of common sense. This, coupled with her logical thought process and intelligence, is revealing itself to us through the deductions she is now making about what she is learning."

"Laken, Bridget's textbook explanation aside, we think Tremble is perfect, too, but that does not preclude her from learning as much as she can. Let's get back to what the Royals can tell her." CeCe winked at Tremble as she took her beverage and sat down on the oversized leather couch in the corner.

"Very well then." Laken seemed oblivious to the awkwardness in the room as he again took them back to rejoin the conversation of the Royal Sisters.

In an instant, the beautiful room in a mansion in Neverwrong appeared. Tremble wondered if she would ever physically visit that same room. Abelia's voice interrupted her thoughts.

"Sisters, I have summoned you here in order for our dear Perpetua to share with you something I think it is time you heard." Abelia paused and looked at each of her sisters. "I know that some of you barely remember our dear parents. It saddens me that the youngest in this room have no memories of their own. It is time that Perpetua and I give you some of ours. Generations to come will need to know what we are about to tell you."

"We love to hear stories of Mama and Papa." Tremble searched her mind to put a name with the lovely face that had just spoken. The name Elsavetta quickly appeared. "I do not understand how you can give us your memories."

"We are going to show them to you. They then will become a part of your memory, too." Abelia nodded at Perpetua. Tremble began to watch as the oldest sister began to whisper.

"Excuse me." The image froze as Dana spoke. "I don't understand what is about to happen."

"Yeah, I'm with Mom. Are we about to see a memory within a memory?"

"Yes, you are correct."

Laken held his hands up and pushed into the air directly in front of him. Tremble was amazed as the room in the mansion grew a little smaller and more distant from them. They could now see portions of the actual room in which they were sitting.

"How did you do that?" Tremble stood up and walked toward the image that was suspended before them. It literally looked like Laken had just pushed it away to one portion of the room. "No, don't explain it now. It is more complicated than we need to get into. I do though want you to explain how we are going to view a memory within a memory. I'm afraid my head is going to explode just trying to process it."

"I would like to tell you there is a simple explanation. There is not. At least, not one that I can explain." CeCe took a sip of her drink. "It may be something that you will be able to explain to us later once you have developed your powers to their full potential. Until then, you said it correctly. This is a memory within a memory. You will now see that memory retrieval is not a new skill in your family. Perpetua and her siblings must have learned how to do it from their parents. So that means that it comes from ancient magic."

"How do you know that these memory examples are true?" Dana passed around a plate of brownies that she had brought from the kitchen.

"I asked that same question, Dana. We cannot be certain. It may be possible for memories to be manipulated. It would require great magic though to alter a memory."

Everyone settled into their seats with beverages and brownies in hand before Laken resumed the memory scene.

"Perpetua will show you our memory of when Mama and Papa told us what we should do if anything happened to them. They tried as best they could to prepare their children for what they must have certainly known was likely to come."

"This memory occurred just a few weeks before our parents were taken."

"You are saying that again. We do not understand what 'taken' means." Verina spoke up as her other sisters nodded in agreement.

"This is very hard to say." Perpetua took a deep breath. A look that Tremble could not decipher crossed Perpetua's face.

"They do not need to hear this."

All eyes shifted to the far left corner of the room. From the shadows, Baldric appeared. His command of the room was instant. Tremble could see love and fear in the looks on his sisters' face. All of them except for Perpetua.

"Yes, they do, Baldric. It is time."

"I am against it. This knowledge shall do nothing but hinder their sleep and haunt their dreams."

"This knowledge shall keep them on guard." Abelia moved to stand beside Perpetua. Baldric was silent as he sat down in a stately high back chair in the corner behind where most of his sisters were sitting. He did not argue further even though the look on his face showed his disapproval.

"Our parents left our home here and ventured outside our safe abode. It was late in the day. Our father detected that the evil was growing closer. While several of you slumbered in an afternoon sleep, they crossed the threshold into the outside. They did not return. Our parents had instructed us never to leave our house in the mountain unless everyone else was already gone. Amadeus and I conferred with Baldric and the three of us decided to send out our loyal servants in search of our parents."

"I do not remember Amadeus either." A tear ran down Verina's eye as she made her pronouncement.

"Our dear brother loved all his sisters so very much."

The look of sadness exchanged between Perpetua and Baldric after she said those words. Tremble surmised that this scene was before they all met Scordato.

"We were frantic that our parents were missing. Even though they had told us that the day might come, our youth and great love for them would not let us believe it. We sent out all of those in our house to look for them. In pairs of two, they went, armed and ready to fight. Hours passed. Days passed. A week passed, and then a month. None ever returned."

Perpetua finally sat down and bowed her head. The weight of her story seemed too much for her to bear. Abelia sat down beside her and took hold of her hand. Raising her head again, she looked directly at Baldric and their eyes locked on one another.

"We had no choice." Baldric spoke in the weakest voice that Tremble had ever heard come from him. "Amadeus and I were only nine years old. Yet, we were the oldest. We had to become the men of the family. We made the decision. We left our home in the mountain."

"Most of you girls were babies or toddlers. Abelia and I huddled you in one room. We kneeled and prayed for hours at a time. Somehow, we knew that our prayers should shift to our brothers.

Our tired and fearful hearts knew that our prayers would no longer help our parents."

"We went out into the world, the world outside of our fortress. Alas, we were babes ourselves, but the choice we had was none. Amadeus and I were the only ones left who knew how to get out of our home. Our fear of going outside was overshadowed by our fear of what we might find there. Our fear was justified." Baldric got up from his seat and began to pace back and forth. "We went down the path that curved around the backside of the mountain. Father had told us that this path led to a small garden filled with roses. He said that he longed to create a beautiful fountain there for our mother with tall stone statues all around it. We had heard mother speak of such a courtyard in her childhood home. We easily found the garden. It was only a short distance from the door we had left."

"Was it beautiful?" Verina's voice was soft considering her boisterous disposition. She was hanging on her brother's every word.

Baldric walked up behind her and gently stroked her hair.

"The garden was as beautiful as I have ever seen. The roses floated all around us in every color imaginable. Their petals glistened like diamonds from the morning dew. The aroma was the most desirable smell I believe I have ever taken in. I was mesmerized, until—"

Tremble heard a whimper from Perpetua and Abelia. Looking in their direction, she could see that their eyes were red with tears.

"Go on, Baldric." Crispina's voice was low for a young woman, but it had a melodious tone similar to Abelia's. "We need to hear what you have to say."

"I was mesmerized until I realized that Amadeus was not be-

hind me. I turned around and saw that there was indeed a fountain in the garden. My father must have created one for our dear
mother. Water, as clear as crystal, flowed from it in abundance.
As I watched the flow, the water turned red, blood red. It was
sickening. The aroma was overwhelming. I called out for Amadeus before I covered my mouth and nose to escape the odor."
Baldric did as he had spoken covering his mouth and nose. He
also began to walk around the room as if he was searching. "I
walked around to the other side of the fountain and saw that
Amadeus' shoulder was visible just behind a large statue. I quickly ran to him."

Baldric stopped. His shoulders sagged. He would have collapsed on the floor were it not for Perpetua and Abelia quickly
jumping up and each grabbing one of his arms. They lowered
him into a chair.

"Amadeus' eyes, their stare was like he was looking at nothing, like he had left his body, like the day—"

Baldric looked at the sisters who were now clutching his
hands. More tears came as they looked away from him and into
the faces of the younger girls who were on the edges of their
seats. The faces showed anticipation and fear.

"I followed Amadeus' gaze and saw the most shocking thing
my eyes have ever seen." Baldric pulled out of the grip of his
sisters and held his head in his hands. "Our dear parents, our
dear parents."

"Take your time, Baldric. These girls must hear. They must
know what we are up against."

A few moments passed. The silence in the room grew louder
until it appeared as if everyone was holding their breath. Slowly,
Baldric raised his head again. His eyes were now the color of
onyx. They shone in a cold, dark stare that made the hairs on

Tremble's arm stand up.

"Our dear parents were turned into stone statues. Their beautiful faces frozen in the pain of transformation." The younger sisters gasped and began to cry. "Mother's hand was outstretched as if she was reaching for someone. Father's arm was raised as if he might have drawn his sword, ready to strike. I let out a scream that turned to a roar of anger. As the realization of what I had seen tore through me, I watched as my brother, my twin, reached out his hand to touch our mother's stone one. Something inside me said that I should stop him. I cried out to him, but it was too late. As Amadeus' hand met our mother's stone one, I saw a shimmer of gray light pass through him. His body shook and turned many colors, before it fell to the ground."

"Oh no, is that how our dear brother died?" Crispina's voice was strong. While not the youngest, she was the shortest of all the sisters with tiny hands and feet to go with her small stature. Her hair was the color of corn silk and fell in ringlets down her back.

"No, my dear, our dear Amadeus died later." Perpetua exchanged a glance with Abelia. "I am sure that his inevitable passing began with this moment that he reached out in love to our dear mother."

"Where did this gray light come from? What was it?" Crispina continued her questioning.

"It came from the depths of evil, from the ones who took them from us and trapped them in their stone graves."

Baldric picked up a crystal vase from the table and slung it toward the wall. Tremble waited for the sound of shattering glass. Hearing none, she looked at the wall and saw the vase suspended in midair. Looking back toward the group, she saw that Perpetua had stopped it and with a flick of her wrist. The vase was floating back through the air to the table it had originated.

"Breaking one of Abelia's beautiful vases will not bring our parents back, Baldric. Release your anger and hurt in less damaging ways."

"I don't understand, Brother." Elsavetta continued the questioning. "Do you know who these evil ones are?"

Baldric let out a sigh that was so large it appeared to shrink his body as he expelled it. Tremble turned to look at Perpetua and carefully watched her face. It was a gray color as if she were falling ill.

"The evil followed us here from the land of our parent's birth. The magic is dark. Everything it touches becomes tainted."

The intensity of Baldric's anger was visible as he uttered the words. Tremble could almost feel it. Her mind drifted a moment as she wondered if indeed she could feel the emotions of her ancestor.

"This is the reason that our parents left that land. There was no one left in the land who had not been touched by the evil. It was like a disease that gradually fills a body until it would overcome it." Abelia walked toward her younger sisters as she spoke. "We have learned from an ancient book that our parents' fate was in fulfillment of a long held legend. 'The virtuous ones shall leave their land to escape the evil therein. Their children shall rise up from their stone graves and form a land of wonder.'"

"Are they still there in stone?" Verina's question was almost a whisper.

"Yes, my dear." Baldric had gained control of his emotions. "I visit them and honor their memory even though my blood runs cold to see the horror of it."

"Can they ever be released from there?" Verina's voice grew stronger.

"The legend says it is possible, but it is hard for us to imagine. It says, 'the virtuous ones can only be freed by a tremble of light from another time.'"

"Stop! Stop the movie!" Tremble stood up and shouted. "Stop this right now."

In a flash, everything before them disappeared. They were back in Andrew's sparse den. Tremble glanced at her mother. Dana looked ashen and scared. Tremble was not scared. She was mad.

"You have got to be kidding me. If this is some sort of cruel joke to see what my tolerance level for ridiculous is, you can stop now."

"Tremble, please calm down." Bridget stood up and moved her arms around in what looked to Tremble to be the motion of a spell.

"What are you doing?"

"Well, I was trying to—"

"She is trying to work a spell to calm you down." CeCe jumped up and began doing the same motions as Bridget.

"What is happening to her?" Dana was on her feet and had a worried mother look on her face. "Someone stop that!"

"What the—" As she looked down at herself, Tremble saw flames of fire coming off her. "I can't be on fire. I don't feel a thing."

"It's your aura." Laken's voice was calm, nonchalant. "Your anger is manifesting itself via your aura. I saw flames come off of Belladonna once like that, but they were actually a blackish silver color."

Tremble was momentarily distracted from her own predicament as she watched the reaction to Laken's last statement pass between CeCe and Bridget. She wished that she had learned how to read minds, as from the look on their faces their conversation must be stellar. Her eyes caught a glimpse of golden orange, and she was back to her own situation.

"No mother wants to see flames coming off her child. Make it stop." Dana was pacing back and forth. "Should I call the fire department?"

Tremble let out a howl of laughter. As if a fire extinguisher had sprayed over her body, the flames extinguished instantly.

"Oh, good. You put it out yourself." Bridget sat down. She looked tired. "It is always best if an aura can be controlled by its own enchanter."

Dana gave Tremble a half smile as she walked out of the room. "I'm going to go make some coffee. I have a feeling we are going to need it."

"Tremble, I realize that what you just saw and heard is very grandiose and unbelievable. I wish I could tell you those were the right words to use to describe it. I wish this was a fiction story that came from deep within the twisted mind of some writer." CeCe walked toward Tremble and pulled her into a hug as they both sat back down on the couch. "I'm afraid that I cannot do that. Marcellus and Claudia met a horrid fate. They were frozen in time, suspended. We really think that the better term is murdered. It is not known if the state they are now in can be reversed."

"They are still like that? This all seems like an old story from a fairytale world."

"Their life was a fairytale, but it went horribly wrong." Laken produced images of a young couple at their wedding. "Much like your own parents, Marcellus and Claudia were a power couple of their time. We have shown you a view of Neverwrong that makes it appear to be a mythical kingdom. The truth is that it is very much like the world you live in here. It looks different to you because the colors are not the same and the way things happen is a little different. Yet, as we have said in the past, this human world is parallel to the magical world. It is the same Earth, just another dimension."

"It is another complicated story, Tremble. Allow Laken to continue. Just accept what he has said for the time being. The magical dimension is close enough that you could touch it, if you knew how."

Tremble furrowed her brow as she thought about what CeCe said. She kept quiet and waited for Laken to continue.

"There is not much known about the land that they came from. The Seven were all so young when they lost their parents. There are few stories that exist. There are volumes in the Library that we think may tell some of the history. Sadly, the spells that protect them are very complicated. We are not sure that even Scordato was able to get into all of them. We do know this. They came from a world that was very advanced, even more so than what you or I know. The advancement was not based on some sort of technology that any of us, mortal or immortal, can imagine. It appears that their people had the ability to create whatever they could imagine in their minds with only a thought. Simple or complex, it did not matter. Good or evil did not matter either."

"This is where the trouble started for Marcellus and Claudia." Bridget spoke as she rose to help Dana serve mugs of coffee. "Perpetua, in her letters, has spoken of her mother telling them stories about how they tried to fight the evil. Apparently many died fighting, including most of Marcellus' and Claudia's respective families."

"Marcellus and Claudia, along with a few others, were able to escape with their children. In doing so, however, their powers were somewhat diminished. It was the price they paid for their—"

"I don't understand, Laken. I thought that The Seven were extremely powerful."

"Indeed. Yet, it was a fraction of their parents' original powers. You shall be one of the most powerful to have ever descended from them. Your power will not touch what your family once had. By leaving their world, they gained their freedom. It made them defenseless when they were followed by the evil of their world."

"This evil that followed them and froze them in stone, did it also go after their children?" Dana sat, curled up in a ball position, on the brown leather loveseat in the corner.

"No, that is one thing that Scordato, Amadeus then, learned when he touched his mother's hand. He received a message— they died so you could live—a phrase he would utter for days thereafter. His health went downhill from then on. Perpetua wrote that it was then Baldric's anger had begun. He blamed himself for the change in Amadeus."

"That doesn't make sense. We heard Scordato accuse his brother of leaving him to die."

"I will not be so bold as to defend Baldric." CeCe interjected. "Keep in mind though that Scordato was filled with years of anger and feelings of abandonment. He sees his story only through his own eyes. Perpetua's version seems to, at least, place some blame on Baldric, but I am not sure that she did not also realize that there were other factors in how Amadeus appeared when they left. You can understand from what we just viewed that something passed into Amadeus. A force of some sort contributed to how he is now versus how he was as a mere boy."

"There's nothing about this story that is simple, is there? I understand now why you want me to learn as much about the history as possible. It is certainly a vast amount of information to try to process." Tremble paused and looked deep into her coffee mug. For a moment, she thought she saw a face staring back at her from the liquid. She blinked her eyes and it was gone. The glimmer looked like the face of Jasmine. "I've forgotten what day this is. How many days until my birthday?" Tremble looked at her mother. Dana closed her eyes and moved her lips as she counted to herself.

"Seven."

"In one week, I will be twenty-one. You need to prepare me to meet Jasmine."

Chapter Six

THE NEXT FEW days passed quickly. From early in the morning until late at night, Tremble was constantly with one of her guardians. Only their roles had changed completely into teachers. Tremble's protection was also in the hands of those who she could not see, those stationed all around their home.

"I feel like I am in prison."

It was the morning of the day before her birthday. Tremble and Bridget had been up since before dawn. She was unsuccessfully trying to master a spell that would allow her to move large objects out of her way.

"This is just like geography. I did not like it, so I could not learn it. I still get the southwestern states mixed up."

"Yes, that is true. You will naturally find those things you do not like more difficult. It is why I keep stressing that you need to accept what you are trying to learn. Quit fighting it and it will become easier. This is not a hard spell in comparison to some you have already mastered."

"I don't see that I will need to be moving much furniture in my search for Jasmine and Forrest."

Bridget was having Tremble test her spell casting abilities on a heavy antique chair that was in one of the guest bedrooms. Tremble hoped that she would not damage it in the process; her mother really liked the chair.

"Tremble, dear, your sarcasm is trying my patience before I have had some of your mother's wonderful coffee. You probably will not be moving any furniture. You might have to move an object that could be hindering your access to where one or both of your parents are located. Or, you might even have to free yourself from somewhere that you might be trapped."

"Somewhere she might be trapped?"

Tremble and Bridget turned around to find Dana at the door with a coffee mug in each hand. Before the aroma had the chance to reach the corner where she stood, Tremble could already taste the rich dark liquid she knew the mug contained. She walked toward her mother, reaching for the steaming mug, like a baby reaching for a bottle.

"Oh, thank you, Dana, I need this so." Bridget drank in a large amount before she resumed speaking. "We hope that Tremble is never trapped. It would be reckless on our part not to teach her how to try to free herself though. Don't you agree?"

"Yes, I suppose you are right. No matter how much we talk about all of this, it still doesn't make it any easier for a mother to hear." Dana sighed and gave them a weak smile. "It is times like now that I feel the closest to Jasmine. I understand more fully how she must have felt as she turned her baby over to us."

Tremble could see CeCe standing at the same doorway that

her mother had a few moments earlier. Her hand also held a mug of coffee. A look exchanged between the two of them.

"Yes, Bridget, I think it is time."

"Close the door behind you then. Put up a detection spell so that we will know if he is close." Bridget motioned for Dana and Tremble to sit down on the bed.

"I believe he is sleeping soundly. Despite the long hours of training Tremble, Laken seems to have time to stay up into early morning playing some of those silly games that Andrew so loved. I do not think I shall ever get the sound of Pac Man dying out of my head."

After closing the door, Tremble watched CeCe take the stance of a karate master and move her arms in similar motions as she whispered a spell that created a bright orange glow that hovered over the door.

"Can you see that, Mom?"

Dana looked at Tremble, quizzically. "See what?"

"She cannot."

"Would any enchanter be able to see that?"

CeCe walked into the middle of the room and toward the large antique chair that Tremble had been trying to move.

"No, a spell is only visible to those an enchanter allows to see it; unless an enchanter has mastered the power of seeing beyond their own magic."

"Seeing beyond their own magic? I don't understand."

"I will be brief since we want to show your mother something very important." CeCe paused and sipped her coffee. "There are many levels in the mastery of magic. Enchantments are not just words and movements with power behind them. There are intricate processes that involve the vast depths of the mind and the infinite secrets of nature. Some enchanters never get past the rudimentary levels, the elementary ones, you might say. They are content to be able to do the showy things and get by with that. Others take the craft more seriously and devote years to perfecting one precise intricate spell."

"CeCe speaks great truth, Tremble. I hope that you have the opportunity to meet some of the enchanters and enchantresses who have truly excelled at the art of magic. Just as you might think of a great musician in this world, such as a cellist, who may devote a lifetime of practice to one piece of music, there are many enchanters who have made it their life's work to not only perfect a known spell, but to create a new one."

"Seeing beyond their own magic involves being not only able to detect the magic of others, but to see the science behind it. The enchanter's personal signature on his or her own work. Laken's magical powers are vast indeed. However, he has not had the opportunity to master how to see into my magic, or in the magic of many of the other protectors."

"But, wouldn't it be important for him to master that since he is supposed to be my main protector?"

"We thought we had more time." Bridget shook her head as she set her empty mug on a side table next to where CeCe was sitting. "We knew that your twenty-first birthday would be a pivotal point. We thought it would be the beginning of our process with you. We didn't think that everything would begin to play out so quickly."

"Don't you trust him?"

Tremble realized that she had asked an awkward question. She instantly felt sparks of magic popping around her. While the effects were not visible, it was as if a storm was passing through the room. Glancing at her mother, she realized that Dana was feeling it, too.

"You have the wisdom of Jasmine. You have her ability to look past the layers of the obvious and into the soul of a situation." CeCe leaned up in her chair a few feet from the foot of the bed that Tremble was sitting on. She stared resolutely at her, never blinking. "Laken was created for you, there is no doubt. It was planned for him to have the genetics of my dear brother combined with the Royal DNA. Those genetics would instill loyalty to a degree that is limitless. We cannot for a certainty say what happened in that laboratory twenty-one years ago. I have no reason to doubt that it did not go as planned. It's just—"

"Tell her, CeCe. No one else will. We must tell her. We must do it for Jasmine."

"We just do not know if it was truly the combined DNA of a Protector and a Royal."

Tremble did not understand. She furrowed her brow and shook her head.

"You think that Belladonna intentionally—"

"I think 'intentional' is a strong word. Coercion is as powerful a tool as magic."

Silence became a blanket on the room as the four lived in their own thoughts. Tremble's mind raced with questions and fears.

"Enough of this for now." Bridget walked toward Dana. "There is something very special that we must show you. Afterward, I want you to think deeply about it. This may hold a key to help Tremble find Jasmine."

CeCe stood and joined Bridget in the middle of the room. They stood across from each other and joined hands.

"What we are about to do is very unique. Most of the memories you have seen so far are from the memories of one of The Seven. We told you that as they began their imprisonment in their eternal portrait homes, they gave complete access to their memories. It was a true unified gift. Even Baldric agreed willingly as he knew that it would one day help his descendants. More precisely, all of them knew that it would help the child who would be born in the fulfillment of Scordato's prophecy. They knew it would help you."

Bridget and CeCe smiled as they nodded in Tremble's direction. Tremble felt a swell of emotion grow inside her.

"Jasmine did not relinquish such. Her memories are still within her own life force viewable only by her choosing. There is one memory that she shared with us and us alone. She gave each of us parts of it. Her orders were precise. All four of us, including you and Dana, have to be together before this memory can appear. We know a little about what it contains. We have not seen it though. It is a one-time gift of knowledge. Pay close attention. Do not interrupt it. We will not be able to conjure it again."

Tremble reached over and took hold of her mother's hand. She dared not look at her. Tremble's heart was racing and she felt a cold prickling rising up her back. She heard Dana take a deep breath as her mother squeezed her hand.

"We're ready." The strength in her voice shocked Tremble.

CeCe and Bridget looked at each other as they each took a firmer grip of the other's hands.

"Jasmine, our eternal friend and Queen of the Kingdom of Neverwrong." CeCe closed her eyes as she began to speak. "We ask you to turn your ears toward our call. Reach deep into your depths of power and allow us to convey the message you entrusted to us so many years ago. Your beautiful one is just a few short hours away from her twenty-first birthday. You will soon release to her the powers you have suppressed so that she may fight the evil that has been a shadow over her life." CeCe grew silent.

"Oh, my beautiful friend, we have missed your warm presence in our lives." Bridget took over speaking. "Our hearts and minds have been heavy with the serious responsibility that you entrusted to us. Your wisdom was vast. Your instincts were true. You chose a mother for your child who had more strength than we could have imagined. Her protection has sustained your daughter. Her unflinching devotion has overcome all of the obstacles that have come into their lives. We are ready to show Dana why she was chosen. We are ready for Tremble to hear the words of the one who gave her birth."

Tremble watched as CeCe and Bridget opened their eyes. Their hands began to glow. At first, the glow was a white light, then, a deep beautiful color that Tremble had never before seen. The color was not blue, it was not purple, it was not green— yet, it was all of these colors and none of them. The light grew until it was a round cylinder around both the women. A funnel of light that had the depth of a wall and the lightness of air simultaneously. Tremble felt Dana draw closer to her. Neither of them let their eyes leave the image before them. The light grew in intensity. It grew until they could no longer see the two women.

Tremble felt her mother's prodding touch. Dana did not make a sound, but pointed to their surroundings. Tremble realized it was more than the viewing of a memory. It was as if they were transported to another world.

The room was ancient and futuristic at the same time. It looked like a room in a fairytale castle with its high ceilings and dark décor. Yet, Tremble also viewed objects around the room that might have easily fit in a science fiction movie. She felt her mother's grip tighten as they both realized that a bed was no longer under them. They were in midair. A moment of fear was replaced with a feeling of safety. They would not fall.

Dana pointed down. Several feet below them was a floor. It was clear, like glass, with a beautiful ocean flowing beneath it. They looked at each other and smiled in delight as they saw the most gorgeous multi-colored fish swimming there.

Breaking her gaze, Tremble looked up and saw that a figure stood across the room next to an ancient heavy-looking door. The figure was dressed in a long, beautiful cloak. It was iridescent black and dark blue. Hundreds of tiny diamonds sparkled from within the fabric. It twinkled even in the low light of the room.

Instantly, their view changed. Tremble and Dana both gasped as they saw the image of the figure moving closer. It appeared to be a woman. The colors around her were a mixture of fuchsia and red, purple and blue. At first, it appeared as if the woman's face was cracking. Tremble soon realized that the woman was emerging from a wall. The layers were so close to her face that it gave the illusion that it was her own skin. Tremble began to see the features of the woman's beautiful face. The woman lowered the hood of her cloak. Tremble smiled as she realized her name was—

"Jasmine." It came out of Dana's mouth as a word of reverence. She turned to her daughter and put her arm around her. "This is your mother."

Logic had already told her this, but the validation from the person who shared that title in her heart caused Tremble to feel the emotion behind it. A strong squeeze from the woman who had raised her brought her back to the reality of why they were there. Tremble needed to focus on gaining knowledge, hearing the message that it took the bonds of two of her guardians to convey.

Tremble began to study Jasmine. Once the multicolored layers of the wall were gone, Tremble could see the woman's alabaster skin and ebony hair. Jasmine wore an intricate headdress that resembled leaves and vines. Ruby red lips reminded Tremble of many fairytales her father had read to her. She found it ironic that she had come from one. Jasmine's hands were resting on top of each other over her heart and she was gazing into a circular object, like a large bowl that stood about three feet off the floor. A blue fog was rising from it with a light glimmering from below. Dana squeezed her arm as Tremble realized that Jasmine had begun to speak.

"I was selfish. I should not have allowed my union with Forrest to produce a child. We were so naïve to think that our love could conquer the greatest evil our world has ever known. I am sorry. I should not have created the fulfillment to the prophecy. I have no doubt that is who I hold within my womb. It is a female child. The firstborn girl in the line of Baldric. A Royal of Neverwrong descended from two of The Seven."

Jasmine lifted her hands and head up toward the ceiling. Tears flowed down her face as she reached for the heavens.

"Creator, forgive me. Forgive my selfishness. I loved this child before her conception. She was in my heart before you placed her in my womb. Do not punish her. I am the one. Her father and I, we are responsible. We deserve the punishment. We are not worthy of this exquisite life we have created. Spare her the vengeance of this evil. Allow her to grow up loved and unharmed. I will do anything, anything, to make that possible."

Jasmine moved away from the bowl. The action revealed that the headdress was indeed made of leaves and vines. It was an unusual color by human standards as there was no green in it, only black. Jasmine gently removed the headdress. The action made her cloak move slightly, revealing the small protrusion of her stomach. Tremble smiled at the knowledge that she was the protrusion. She had been at this place before. She was shocked as she watched Jasmine move back to the bowl and immerse the headdress into the foggy blue liquid it contained. As she pulled it out again, it was changed. The black of the vine and leaves was replaced with shimmering silver and white. As if it was kissed with the sparkle of a thousand clear jewels, the shine from the headdress was almost blinding.

"I shall surrender my daughter to another mother. She shall have what she herself cannot create. I shall sacrifice for my self-ishness. I shall not know the joy of the childhood of this one." Jasmine held up the headdress. It now looked more like a crown. "This shall lead my daughter back to me."

A crack of thunder made Tremble jump. In a blink, they were back in the bedroom. Tremble looked around and found Dana in the center of the room, hugging CeCe and Bridget. Slowly, she turned and faced Tremble.

"I know how to find Jasmine. I've had your ticket back to her all along." Dana turned back to the other two women. "I cannot believe that I forgot about it all of these years."

CeCe and Bridget looked exhausted. Their normally healthy complexions were ashen and pale.

"You were not supposed to remember, not until now. None of us knew this secret. I sincerely doubt that even Belladonna knows about what we just saw."

Dana tried to run out of the room. She bounced back as if she had hit a rubber wall.

"Oh, I am so sorry."

CeCe moved toward Dana. With a flick of her wrist, CeCe removed the shield that was blocking the exit. Dana quickly left the room. It appeared to Tremble as if the shield reappeared after her mother left.

"What's going on? I don't understand." Tremble watched as both CeCe and Bridget laid down on the bed. "Are you two okay?"

"Yes, Tremble. This experience was very taxing on our systems. There was a great deal of magic expended to bring out that memory." Bridget rose back up. "CeCe, Dana will not be able to get back into the room."

"Oh, yes, I forgot."

CeCe sat up, snapped her fingers on both hands, and made a movement that reminded Tremble of an umpire's ruling of safe. She immediately stretched back on the bed.

"How did it feel to see such an intimate moment with Jasmine?" Bridget had propped two pillows behind her and was sitting up in the bed.

"I can't even begin to describe it. I realize that I should be dripping in the reality of all of this. All of you have given me too many reasons not to understand the magnitude of it. It just seems like something that I should be reading in a book, and not as part of my genealogy."

Before Bridget could reply, Dana rushed back into the room carrying what looked to Tremble like a jewelry box. Everyone sat up at attention.

"Several weeks before you were born, Jasmine asked me to come over to her apartment one afternoon. Your father was on a long shift at the hospital. We had a wonderful afternoon. We talked about all sorts of things. We ate lots of food. I even introduced her to some of Andrew's favorite music. We danced and danced." Dana paused for a moment. Her face was lit up with the laughter of the memory. "It was getting late. I knew she was tired. I was getting ready to leave when she asked me to wait. She had something to give me. She went into her bedroom. In a few minutes, she returned with this box. Jasmine said that it was a very special piece of family jewelry. She wanted me to give it to you on a very special occasion, like your wedding day. I have to admit that I was more thrilled that she thought I would still have you then, than to think about what it might really be. Now, I know what it is really for." Dana opened the lid of the box. It contained the beautiful silver and white headdress that Jasmine had pulled from the smoky bowl. "It will help you find Jasmine."

Tremble reached out to touch the beautiful headpiece.

"Stop!"

Everyone turned. Laken was standing in the doorway, in his Superman pants.

"What are you doing and why wasn't I invited?"

"Laken, calm down." CeCe got off the bed and walked toward him. "We've been sharing things with Tremble this morning about Jasmine."

"And, why didn't you wake me? I need to know everything that Tremble does."

Tremble caught a look between CeCe and Bridget. From the look on his face, it appeared that Laken saw it, too.

"Wait a minute. I came to the kitchen about an hour ago. All I saw was half a pot of coffee. I did not see or hear any of you. I thought you might have gone out shopping." Laken looked around the room. "You have been in here all along. You put up something to keep me out." His eyes darted to each of them before they rested on CeCe. "You don't trust me. Your own flesh and blood."

"Laken, it is not as black and white as that."

"Perhaps not, but it will be. I'm contacting Belladonna immediately."

"No, you will not."

"I most certainly will. You cannot stop me."

"I certainly can. I am your superior officer, for one thing. I am also not only your aunt, but also the person who gave birth to you. To use a very human phrase—I brought you into this world, I can take you out."

"I only answer to Belladonna."

"You ultimately answer to Belladonna. In human time, you answer to me. I have my reasons for only sharing certain things with Tremble. You will need to accept that, or else."

"Else, what?" Laken's eyes glowed with anger.

"Or else you shall be banished."

"CeCe! Watch your words." Bridget was off the bed and standing between CeCe and Laken before Tremble knew what was happening.

"Belladonna would never allow it." Laken's tone of anger changed to smugness. "I am like her own son."

"Ah, but you are not. Tremble is, however, her niece. She is the only child of her only sibling. Belladonna will do whatever it takes to protect her. You, my dear nephew, need to chill out and sit down. You need to remember that you are but a child yourself. A child given a man's job. You will not cross us, Laken. Your father died protecting Tremble. You will honor his memory by doing what you are told."

Tremble was not sure if he was giving up or going to make a very long distance phone call. Either way, Laken turned and left the room. CeCe started to go after him. Bridget stopped her in her tracks.

"You have done enough. Calm down, or I will be the one calling Belladonna." Bridget's eyes were stone cold and her tone was dead serious. CeCe stopped moving and Bridget started to leave the room. "I am very sorry that you had to witness this outburst. Emotions are running high these days."

Bridget left. Tremble and Dana were silent. At some point during the argument, Dana had closed the box and was holding it on her lap. Tremble did not have a desire to touch the headpiece any longer.

"This is all a mess. I am causing too much anxiety. I should have been named Trouble instead of Tremble."

"Ridiculous. I let my temper get the best of me. Laken has received too much coddling from Belladonna. Anton would not be happy with how he is acting. We have very strict training at the Bureau. You do not question a superior officer, even if you are the Protector assigned to the heir to Neverwrong. There is one thing he is right concerning. You probably should not touch the headpiece until you are ready to use it. The magic attached to it is very strong. It will probably set you on a path that you cannot undo."

"Did you know that Jasmine had created it?" Dana seemed content to keep possession of the now precious item.

"No, I did not. I doubt anyone did, perhaps not even Forrest. Jasmine knew that there might be a future situation where it might be best that no one but herself had that knowledge. There are forms of magical torture that involve permanently extracting memories. Strong enchanters like your parents could counteract them if they were not compromised in some way. If they did not have complete use of their powers though, it could be disastrous. This memory was obviously firmly attached to her daughter. It would give someone with an evil agenda a definite advantage in locating you."

"Why is that?" Dana was still clutching the box.

"Mom, I think you could set that down beside you."

Dana ignored Tremble and focused on CeCe, waiting for an answer.

"Jasmine was pregnant when she worked this spell that protects it. Because of that, Tremble is part of the spell."

"What?" Tremble's voice rose a decibel.

"I'm not sure how to explain this. I have not had that much experience with pregnant enchantresses." CeCe paused and lines appeared in her forehead as she thought about what she would say. "From my own experience, when I was carrying Laken—"

"Oh, I really can't wrap my mind around that." Tremble shook her whole body. She saw multi-colored sparks flying from her.

"Sorry, can't help it. Anyway, when an enchantress is carrying a child, they are helping the child grow their magic, just like the physical growth that occurs. It makes you connected, genetically and magically. Jasmine would have no problem finding you wherever you were. Her magical sense would locate you."

"Does it work the other way?"

"What do you mean?"

"You are saying it works from mother to child. What about child to mother?"

"Well, I really hadn't thought about it from that perspective."

"Because if it does—"

"If it does, you should not have any trouble finding Jasmine." CeCe headed toward the doorway. "When Laken calms down, we just might have to do an experiment."

Chapter Seven

"SINCE WE DON'T know what tomorrow will bring, literally."

Dana began the conversation as everyone had migrated to the kitchen around lunchtime. The rest of the morning had been quiet. Emotionally exhausted, Tremble had gone back to bed and snuggled with her neglected companion, Choo Choo. She also had a brief phone conversation with VeVette. Her best friend seemed to be growing very suspicious of the changes in Tremble's life. She had no idea what type of excuse she would give her when she had to go off in search of her parents. Tremble thought she just might have to ask someone to give her a spell for that.

"I thought it might be a good idea for Tremble and I to go out this evening to dinner to celebrate her birthday. Despite all of the magical crazy that is going on and the dangerous crazy that might be in the future, I want to celebrate this milestone in my daughter's life. I want us to have this memory. I do not mean to be rude, but you three are not invited."

"That is perfectly understandable, Dana. I wholeheartedly agree—"

"Has everyone lost their minds?" Laken interrupted Bridget. "Have you not forgotten the danger that Tremble is in?"

"Young man, we had a talk this morning. I thought we came to an understanding. I will not throw threats at you as CeCe did. I will call Belladonna. Your behavior better shape up or we will ship you out."

Total silence filled the room. Even CeCe had a shocked look on her face. After Bridget's earlier reaction to CeCe's dialogue with Laken, no one expected Bridget to be taking a similar stance.

Tremble closely watched Laken. She was beginning to notice that his humility was fading and his strength and deviance was growing. She knew she should be on guard, yet, something about the change in him made her feel a little safer. If she was honest with herself, she knew that the attraction she was beginning to feel was far more dangerous than whatever might be brewing in his head. Tremble was not the best at concealing her own feelings.

"Tremble and her family have been in danger her entire life. That is a fact. In reality, the first couple of years of her life were probably the most dangerous as it was more common knowledge in our world that a royal birth had occurred. Jasmine's aura was still detectable during that first year. Dana has given Tremble the unconditional love and protection that only a mother could. We will not deny her this private celebration. Our protection forces will be in place as they always have been. We do not have to sit at the table with them."

Laken's jaw tightened, yet he nodded his head in agreement.

Catching his eye, Tremble saw a twinkle and wondered if he had just been privy to her thoughts.

"Thank you, Bridget. That means a lot to me. I trust that you can make your own dinner plans. I have also arranged for Tremble and I to have manicures and pedicures this afternoon before our dinner, and perhaps a little shopping." Dana smiled as she turned to Tremble. "Birthday girl, you need to get yourself upstairs after you finish that sandwich and get ready. We are going to have a wonderful afternoon."

FOUR HOURS LATER, Tremble and Dana were leaving their favorite day spa with colorful and pampered fingers and toes.

"It's a magical feeling, isn't it?" Tremble caught what she had said and let out a huge giggle. "Oh, my, I must have gotten so relaxed I forgot I was a witch."

"Bridget would not appreciate you referring to yourself with that term. It's enchantress, remember."

"Enchantress, samantress. I still can't get the image of Samantha Stephens out of my head." Tremble looked into the windows of the quaint shops they passed while walking to their restaurant.

"You watched too much television as a child. The enchantresses I have met through the years could work magic circles around that TV witch. I agree with Bridget. A stereotype needs overcoming. The whole evil cauldron thing, too. If you want to emulate Hollywood witches, I would suggest the ones from *Practical Magic*."

"Who put the lime in the coconut?" They both sang simultaneously and broke into laugher.

"Oh, by the way, before we go into the restaurant, I have one more surprise for you."

"Okay, this birthday girl is loving your surprises today."

Before they went to the spa, they stopped at Tremble's favorite dress shop and purchased new outfits, including shoes, for each of them. They had changed into them before they left the spa.

"I hope you love this one. It was a risk on my part." Dana paused at the door of Tremble's favorite restaurant. It was called "The Waterfall." It specialized in Polynesian food. "I've invited VeVette to join us."

"Oh, okay, well that is a surprise. It is a great one though. I would love to see her. It has been forever. This will be fun."

"And, I also invited Jake."

"What? Jake? He's supposed to have gone back to wherever he was stationed."

"Yes, that's true. With everything going on, I have not had a chance to tell you everything I knew about him and his family. Jake's grandfather died, Sylvia's father. He was ill for about a year, gradually declining. Since Jake was already home on leave, he was allowed to stay an extra week to attend the funeral. It was yesterday. We sent food and flowers. The funeral was two hours away in Chesterfield. Sylvia is staying for a couple of weeks with her mother. Jake came home last night. He has to leave tomorrow."

"Oh, Mom, this is going to be awkward. I am very sorry about his grandfather. I just don't know what to do about Jake."

"I want you to listen to me." Dana took Tremble by the shoulders and looked her straight in the eyes. "If none of this had happened; if you had no idea that you were an enchantress with this horrible prophecy hanging over you, what would you do about Jake? Would you give him another chance?"

"If I didn't have this whole magical thing in my history, I don't think we would be having this discussion. Jake would not have left like he did."

"And?"

"And we would still be together." Tremble sighed and smiled. "Okay, you win. I need to just give in and have dinner with all the people I love who are still here to love." An understanding look passed between them.

"That's absolutely right. Now, come on, I'm starving."

"I'M NOT JOKING! My history professor looks just like Hitler. It is majorly spooky. We had to cover a chapter on the Holocaust, and I thought the whole class was going to die. He doesn't seem to know that he bears such a striking resemblance." VeVette was giving an animated account about her most recent year in college.

"That story is harder to believe than the one about your suite-mate being a belly dancer." Jake shook his head as he laughed.

Tremble had found herself smiling and staring at the both of them several times throughout the evening. The four-course Polynesian meal offered lots of time for stories and laughter. It felt so wonderful to be with them again. It saddened her to real-ize that it would soon be over. Tremble wondered when, if ever, she would experience a night like this again.

"Jake, do you know how long you will be overseas?" Dana turned the conversation in a different direction as they were waiting for their desserts.

"Well, Mrs. Dawson, that depends on several things. First of all, I really can't discuss the mission."

"We understand. Top-secret government stuff. Everyone has

secrets these days."

Tremble could not believe how brazen her mother was with such comments. Dana gave her a wink as Tremble looked in her direction.

"We call it classified. My unit will be on the front line. There is certainly an extra level of danger to that. But, the way I look at it, everything we do has a dangerous side."

Tremble kicked her mother under the table as Dana began to speak.

"Ouch. Yes, even sitting in this nice restaurant is dangerous."

"Exactly." Jake seemed oblivious to what had occurred. Ve-Vette seemed to be taking it all in. "We are in a public place. It could be robbed or there could be a fire, or even a terrorist attack."

"Not at The Waterfall. It is a Polynesian Palace—an escape to the islands." VeVette was pointing at the sign that hung on the wall behind them. Tremble laughed. VeVette had great timing for sarcasm.

"We hear way too often these days about all sorts of accidents and freak events happening everywhere. Not to mention the general craziness that goes on in this world in general. I could just as easily be hit by a bus on Main Street as I could be injured on the front line."

"I've already heard this speech. This is a rerun. You are the Man of Steel. We all remember." Tremble was laughing until she saw the look on Jake's face. For some reason, something seemed to have changed. He looked at his watch.

"You know, Mrs. Dawson, I really appreciate you including me in your special night for Tremble. I am honored that you thought of me. Time has flown by, but I need to be up and ready to go before the sun rises. I think I will say goodnight. Before you try to argue, I have already taken care of the bill. It's my present to Tremble." Jake rose from the table.

"Jake, you haven't even had your dessert yet? What's wrong?" Tremble searched his face to see an inkling of what changed his demeanor.

"I'm sorry, Tremble. Duty calls." Jake leaned down and kissed her on the cheek. "Happy Birthday. I love you."

Before she could say a word, he was hugging Dana and Ve-Vette and scurrying out the door. At that moment, a group of wait staff walked up to the table carrying a flaming volcano cake and singing "Happy Birthday."

"Go on, Tremble. Go after him."

Tremble ran toward the door. Once out on the sidewalk, she looked in both directions, but Jake was nowhere in sight. On a hunch, she went toward the parking lot on the right of the building. Several rows back, she saw him getting into a vehicle.

"Jake! Wait! I want to talk to you!" She could see him hesitate before he got in. She made it to the door before he put it in gear. "Stop! Please!" Tremble banged on the driver's side window. He got out of the car.

"Tremble, I know it is your birthday, and I'm sorry that it turned out this way. I guess I should have listened to my own instincts and not come."

"Then, why did you?" Tremble felt her defenses rising.

"I thought that since your mother invited me that you were okay with it. I thought that it was a sign that maybe we had a chance. I guess I was dreaming."

"I don't understand, Jake. What happened back there? I thought we were having a great time."

"Yes, a great time." Jake ran his fingers through his hair. Tremble recognized it as an old habit from when lots of hair adorned his head. "Then your mother got serious for a minute, and I tried to diffuse that. I realized though that I did not have to do that. It doesn't seem to concern you that I am going into a war zone."

"You are the one who joked the other night about being the Man of Steel."

"Yes, Tremble, I did. The girl I used to know would have recognized that joking about something serious is one of my defense mechanisms. The girl I used to know would have been worried about me anyway."

"There's one thing for certain, Jake. You might as well know it now. I am not the same girl you used to know." As the words came out of her mouth, Tremble realized the weighty truth of them. She longed to tell this man all her secrets.

"I gathered that. I guess I am not the same person either. You have a new life. I know it will be fabulous and I meant what I said in there. I love you Tremble. Somehow, I don't think that will ever change." He gave her a short smile and got back into the car.

A thousand emotions surged through her. She could feel the sparks leaving her fingertips. If she let him go, she might not ever see him again. One or both of them might not survive the battles they faced. From deep within her, she heard a voice. She was not sure if it was her own conscience or one of the many who watched over her. The voice simply said, "Tell him."

She walked around to the passenger side of the car, opened the door, and got in.

"I've got something to tell you. It's better than any of VeVe's stories."

"TREMBLE, THAT'S AN incredible story. Most guys would say it was the best excuse they ever heard for breaking up. I am not most guys. My mind cannot even begin to decipher what you are telling me. I have always known you had some special something that made you different from every other girl I have ever met. I thought it was pure love on my part. Maybe magic would explain that sparkle that has always drawn me like a moth to a flame."

An hour passed before Tremble was finished telling the new story of her life. She used Jake's cell phone to call her mother to explain that Jake would take her home in a little while.

"Oh, Jake, stop being mushy. There's no sparkle to my story now. It's all very dim and dangerous. If I do not fight this Scordato, the Kingdom of Neverwrong will cease to exist. It has been prophesied that the heir will forsake her homeland. There doesn't seem to be too much confidence in my ability to overcome this force."

"I suppose that my reaction should be to tell you to let the prophecy come true. Stay right here, safe and sound, and forsake your homeland." Jake took Tremble's hand in his own, squeezing it tight. Tremble missed that feeling. "That's not who we are though. We have always dreamed of doing something that is bigger than we are. I admit I did not expect to be going half way around the world to do it. I would not have imagined that you would be going to another world. Before I settle into a job, a mortgage, and three kids, I want do something that is beyond that suburban normal we know. I want to touch something and leave an impression. Even without all that you have told me, I think you want the same thing too." Jake laughed and shook his head. "I just never imagined that you would have something so—"

"Unbelievable, outrageous, shocking."

"You know, somehow it isn't in a way. Now, that I think about it, I think your father tried to prepare me for this in a small way."

"What?"

"After we had been dating a couple of years, you remember when I went on that golfing trip with your dad and his doctor buddies?"

"Yes, you went to Myrtle Beach. I was really not happy because I didn't get to go."

"It was right before your dad got sick. It was a great trip. One evening, he and I went for a walk on the beach. We talked about all sorts of things. He told me that something might happen to you in the future that would be hard to believe. He told me that no matter what, I had to remember that you were the same Tremble I knew right then. He said that it would be out of your control, but that you would have to face it."

"That sure does sound like Dad. I would give anything if he was here to help me through this."

"He is here, Tremble. He is right there inside of you. You are just as much Andrew and Dana Dawson as you are the other two. What are their names again?"

"Jasmine and Forrest."

"Do they have last names?"

"Ah, I don't know." Tremble chuckled as she thought about his question. "I haven't heard any last names."

"You must be true royalty then. I don't know what Queen Elizabeth's last name is either."

Jake paused and looked straight ahead, gazing into the distance. It gave Tremble a chance to stare at his profile. She wanted it imbedded in her memory.

"Your father is with you, Tremble, and so am I. I want to be in your life, all of it."

Tremble answered him with a kiss, long and intense. There were tears on her cheek when it was over. She had missed him.

"HE JUST ACCEPTED it. He did not seem shocked or scared. Jake just took me in his arms and accepted everything I told him. I offered to show him some of the spells I have learned. He said it was not necessary. When I did though, his eyes were as big as saucers." Tremble went straight for her mother's room when she came home later that night. "Bridget will be so proud. I was able to levitate Jake's car."

"Tremble that was a dangerous thing to do. You could have damaged it or someone could have seen you."

"It was the only thing I could think of that could really show him that I could do magic."

"You have got to be careful. Couldn't you have made something appear in the car?"

"I was so anxious for him to understand that I didn't think of the consequences. There wasn't anyone around that I could see and I didn't make it rise very far, just far enough."

Tremble smiled to herself as she remembered how Jake clutched the steering wheel. She giggled as she wondered if he thought he was going to have to drive it in the air.

"It made you feel good to tell him, didn't it?"

"Yes, it did. It made it seem more real to me by telling someone normal. Jake said that he thought Dad had tried to prepare him by hinting that there might be something that would happen to me in the future that would be hard for him to believe."

"That sounds like Andrew, thinking ahead. He thought a lot

of Jake. He trusted him. I do, too. We never shared our secret with anyone. We knew that if anything ever happened to your father or me, the guardians would take over and you would probably disappear from life here. Andrew said many times that he hoped you would not lose Jake and VeVette. That somehow the guardians would allow you to stay connected to them."

"If something happens and I go away and don't come back, will you please explain it all to VeVette?" Tremble snuggled next to her mother in Dana's king size bed.

"Oh, Tremble, don't talk that way. You will come back, I need you."

"I know you need me, Mom. I need you more than you can imagine. I am going up against something that neither one of us can really imagine even despite what we have already seen. The grim reality is that it might win. Jasmine's careful planning and protection may be for naught. I may not be powerful enough or a strong enough warrior. What I am saying? I'm not a warrior at all."

"Stop this stressing. Go change into your nightclothes. I want you to sleep with me tonight. I want you snuggled beside me as you pass into your twenty-first year of life. Whatever comes tomorrow, we will face together. Tonight, you are still my little girl."

"TREMBLE, DANA, I think you better wake up."

Tremble stretched her legs out in the bed and kicked at the covers as she slowly opened her eyes. The room looked very bright. She turned to see her mother doing the same.

"What's wrong, Laken?" Tremble sat up in the bed and looked around. "Where is all that light coming from?" She heard a gasp as she turned and looked at her mother.

"Oh, my, Laken, what does this mean?"

Dana pulled the bed covers away from Tremble. As she looked down at her own body, Tremble realized why her mother's look was so strange. A soft lavender glow appeared to be oozing from her every pore.

"Happy Birthday, Tremble!"

Bridget came through the door behind Laken. The most beautiful birthday cake Tremble had ever seen was floating through the room toward her in front of Bridget. It was every shade of purple imaginable and was as tall as Tremble with luscious icing and decorations synchronized to the music that was coming from it. Tiny butterflies of all sorts of iridescent colors flew through the air around her as a shower of glistening sparkles fell like rain from above. Tremble thought she was living a fairytale and expected to hear someone say, "bippity bobbity boo" at any moment.

"That's indescribable! I cannot even think of the words, it is so beautiful. It tastes like the icing has lavender in it."

"That would be correct. It was my mother's recipe." Bridget was in full bubble, reminding Tremble of a fairy godmother who might have said the phrase she was waiting for.

"You have a mother?"

"Well, of course, I have a mother, Tremble. Most beings do." Bridget laughed and shook her head. "I see you have received your adult aura. Let us see how your powers are progressing. Can you tell what the flavor of the cake is?"

"That is her adult aura? Will it stay that bright?" Dana seemed concerned about the light Tremble was emitting.

"No, it will not, but she now needs to be the one to tone it down. We will show her the techniques. CeCe is especially good at this since her aura color is often the color of her mood, black."

Tremble saw a sleepy looking CeCe making faces at the back of Bridget's head.

"I can see that." Bridget continued to follow the cake as it moved closer to the bed. "Answer my question, birthday girl. What's the flavor of the cake?"

Tremble closed her eyes and tilted her head to the right. She knew that like most magical abilities, she would have better success if she relaxed her mind and allowed it to *pick up* the signals on its own. Her mouth began to water as it encountered the lavender icing first.

"The icing has an earthy, but elusive flavor. It's on the tip of my tongue, and then the sweetness touches it and it is gone again."

"What a beautiful description, Tremble." Bridget's voice was reaching a high pitch of excitement. "You could write descriptive copy for culinary magazines."

Tremble raised an eyebrow at the comment, but did not open her eyes. She could feel an icy, vibrating feeling as she thought she was encountering one of the decorations.

"That decoration is alive. It's vibrating and cold."

"I wondered how you would react to that." CeCe sounded as if she was enjoying Tremble's exploration. "It is a popular decoration in our world called blimbets. They are created magically for the purpose of decoration and could be compared to frozen sparklers."

"Only you can eat them." Laken interjected into the conversation making Tremble open that one eye again.

"I think I will love them. Mom, you should have let them create a cake for me when I was little. VeVette would have freaked out."

Tremble closed the eye again and allowed her mind to leave the lavender icing and blimbets behind and reach the cake.

"I'm getting conflicting signals here, but I have to be honest, Bridget. I'm going to be ticked if it isn't chocolate."

Tremble breathed deeply and began studying the cake again. The texture was moist and rich. There was a hint of a citrus flavor.

"Orange."

Then came the dark rich earthy sweetness that she craved almost daily.

"Dark chocolate orange cake with lavender frosting. Oh, my, I can't wait to taste it for real."

Tremble opened her eyes and saw that the blimbets were dancing. It reminded her of fireworks. She looked down at herself. The soft lavender glow of her aura had changed into a rich deep purple.

"What's happening to me now?"

"I think the change in color could be signaling that you are happy. We hope that is the case." Bridget came up to the side of the bed that Tremble was sitting on and engulfed her in a big hug CeCe was close behind her. "Happy birthday, dear girl. This is a most special day in your life. It is special in ours as well. We both hoped that we would be here to see you cross into adulthood."

"Bridget, CeCe, if Andrew were here, he would say this far better than I will." Dana paused as she wiped a tear from her face. "There have been so many guardians in Tremble's life. We lost count of them all. You two have been steadfast throughout our entire journey. It was always comforting to me to know that you had my back. I knew that Jasmine, and I suppose Belladonna as well, only chose the best ones to protect our daughter. I thank you for all you have done."

"It's been a pleasure to be of service." CeCe answered with a bow as Bridget moved out of the way so that CeCe could hug Tremble. "It has truly been a labor of love."

Tremble looked toward the corner of the room. Laken was sitting in a chair and was looking down at his arms; a dark emerald green color was taking over his aura. It reminded Tremble of the Wicked Witch of the West. As if he could feel her watching him, he looked up. She caught her breath, for a moment, she saw that his eyes looked green, too.

"Ah, let us not forget that there's another person with a birthday today. Yes, it was not too long after Tremble's birth in this world that Laken was born in Neverwrong." CeCe walked over and reached down to embrace him. "Are you still mad at me for counseling you?"

Laken stood up and moved into CeCe's embrace. Tremble wondered if he had grown overnight, as she did not remember him towering so much over CeCe. His eyes no longer glowed green. Perhaps it was just a reflection from his aura.

"Your cake shall come later in the day." Bridget made Tremble's cake stop moving. Beside her, a table appeared with plates, forks and a tray of beverages.

"My cake? I didn't expect a cake."

"Of course, you shall have a cake; it is your twenty-first birthday, as well. We shall enjoy yours this evening. Too much cake at once would be—"

"There is no such thing as too much cake." Tremble chimed in with a big smile. Up until that point he had been solemn, now Laken's eyes lit up with laughter before the emotion reached his mouth in a smile as well. "Happy Birthday, Laken. Our first birthday together. Come help me eat my cake."

The room grew silent as Bridget began serving. She did not

do it the traditional way.

"Bridget, I am surprised that you are using magic to do this."

Dana and Tremble had slipped out of the room to brush their teeth and do other morning things as the others had found seats and waited for the cake. Tremble was amazed to find that Bridget was sitting in a corner chair herself. She appeared to be instructing the cake to cut itself into slices. She then pointed for those slices to fly to the plates. It was a whirlwind of activity.

"Dana, my dear, there is no denying our magical abilities now. What better time than our Tremble's birthday to embrace them again? Of course, we shall refrain from this type of activity when we are out in the mortal world. CeCe and I both feel that it is only appropriate for Tremble to begin to see, and to use, magic in her day-to-day life for as long as she is still in this world. She needs to get used to seeing it and using it. If she stares in amazement, as she is doing right now, when she is in Neverwrong, everyone will know that she is not a 'native,' so to speak."

Tremble looked up from her plate, as she was about to take her first bite. The blimbets were popping and glowing.

"What do you mean?"

"There's magic everywhere in Neverwrong." CeCe settled in a cross-legged position on the opposite edge of the bed from Dana. "It's a magical world, so everyone is constantly using magic to go about their day."

"I get that part. It is the 'not a native' part that I do not understand. I thought that the people of Neverwrong would recognize me. From the way you have described the prophecy and how the Royals are held in such reverence, I thought that Belladonna's photo was on money or something."

"Your appearance has been anticipated. There is no doubt about that." Laken rose as a plate of cake came flying in his direction. "But, no one, outside of Belladonna and those who have been protecting you, knows anything about your appearance. Even I only saw a few images of you through the years. I spent my whole life up until now dreaming about what you would look like."

All eyes went to Laken as he made his last statement. Tremble saw so much devotion in his eyes that she was embarrassed. He lowered his eyes, as his coloring revealed that he too felt that way.

"Tremble, this is one of the aspects of entering the magical world that will be in your favor—no one will know who you are. We will teach you today how to tone down your aura. We will cloth you in the attire of Neverwrong. With the invisibility skills you have mastered so expertly, you should blend into Neverwrong and any other magical world that you have cause to enter."

Tremble took the waiting bite of her cake. The flavors exploded in her mouth like a symphony performance.

"Oh, oh, that is the best cake, I have ever—" She did not allow herself to finish the sentence as she consumed another bite. It was like an out-of-body experience. Tremble felt like she was floating. She glanced over at her mother and saw that Dana too was rolling her eyes in pure enjoyment.

"What is in this?" Dana mumbled between bites.

"Well, you might say that magical ingredients have a little extra special something." Bridget gave Dana a wink, as she began to eat her own slice.

"You will find that everything cooked with magic is more than it is the mortal way—sweeter, more savory, richer, and more delicious." CeCe made a purring sound as she ate another bite.

"More is more. That's what my mother always said." Dana sighed with delight as she took another bite.

"Yes, Belladonna, I read you." CeCe suddenly put down her plate and spoke into a device on her wrist. "We are with Tremble and Dana now. We were having some birthday—" CeCe glanced over at Bridget. "Yes, we will do that and be ready in fifteen minutes. Goodbye."

"Well, I guess the party's over." Tremble quickly began to finish her cake.

"Belladonna would like to speak with all of us as soon as possible. Let's all assemble in the living room in fifteen minutes."

Laken was the first to leave the room, quickly followed by CeCe. Dana went into her bathroom as Bridget began cleaning up the plates and such from the cake with a few flicks of her wrist. Before Tremble could thank her, the cake disappeared.

"Oh, no, it's gone."

"Oh, my dear, do not fret." Bridget gave Tremble a quick hug as she led her out of the room. "I can bring that cake back in two seconds or another one of your own special order."

"I loved it, Bridget. I appreciate you doing that for me. It was a special birthday surprise."

"I'm afraid we will not be able to give you much to make this day as wonderful as it should be for you. So, let's eat cake as much as we can."

Tremble left Bridget and continued to walk down the hallway to her own room. Closing the door behind her, she collapsed face down into her own bed. She was exhausted in every way possible. Realizing that time was quickly ticking by, she rose and headed to her bathroom. Looking at herself in the mirror, she noticed that the purple streaks in her hair had turned a deeper color overnight and that her complexion was glittering.

"I guess I am a grown up witch, I mean enchantress, now."

As Tremble talked to her reflection, her mind drifted to the world of information that had been poured into her over the past few weeks. She turned the shower on and as she waited for the water to heat up, Tremble wondered if she would ever again have a normal day.

"I HAVE RECEIVED a message from Jasmine. It is the first I have gotten in several years. The relief is considerable, as you can well imagine."

Belladonna had been speaking to Laken in hushed tones when Tremble and Dana had arrived in the living room. CeCe was pacing in the back of the room as Bridget sat on the couch. No one looked happy. It was Belladonna's first statement to the group. There was not any greeting.

Tremble started to speak, but Laken came up behind her and took hold of her arm. She did not know how he got to her so quickly.

"Our suspicions have been confirmed. Scordato has entrapped Forrest somewhere. We believe that he could be trapped within the mountain."

"That is not surprising. Why wouldn't Scordato use the area he is most familiar with and that we know the least about?" CeCe stopped pacing and walked toward the screen. She turned to Tremble. "In the years since The Seven have passed into their portrait state, few of their descendants have physically ventured to the mountain. It is easier and safer for them to go as we took you, in a virtual sense."

"You have taken Tremble to the Library? Was she able to open the sacred volumes?" Belladonna stood up and Tremble saw that she was dressed as if she might have stepped out of a

James Bond movie. A formfitting silver leather jumpsuit could have easily allowed her to run on a high-speed chase after the bad guy.

"We have not gotten that far yet, Your Royal Highness." Laken walked back into Belladonna's view. "We thought that after today, things might be different for her success."

"Yes, today, it is a day of transformation. Congratulations on reaching your twenty-first year, Tremble. And Happy Birthday to you as well, Laken." The only smile Belladonna seemed to be able to force was for her prodigy.

"Get back to Jasmine. What was her message? How was it communicated?" Tremble was not going to waste any time on pleasantries with Belladonna.

"That's what I was hoping you might offer us some enlightenment on."

Belladonna looked straight at Tremble. Her hard gaze began to soften as she looked deeply into Tremble's eyes. It began to give Tremble an uneasy feeling, so she cut her eyes toward Laken. He had a puzzled look on his face.

"Her message was mainly about you."

"Your Highness, you sound as if that surprises you." Laken's sudden comment broke Belladonna's gaze on Tremble.

"Well, no, not really. Of course, she is concerned about her daughter. The message just sounds as if they have been communicating. You have told me of dreams that Tremble has had, but not of any direct communication."

"There has been none." From behind her, Tremble could hear Bridget clear her throat. "What did Jasmine say?"

"She said that she knew that all had been revealed to Tremble and that what you are planning is correct. Jasmine also said that Dana would know where Tremble could find her." Belladonna began looking into the room as if she was searching. Dana stood up and walked toward the screen.

"She said that I would know? I do not understand."

"Jasmine said that it had something to do with a gift that she gave to you for Tremble and the conversation that you had about it."

Bridget started coughing loudly, so much so that everyone looked in her direction. "I'm sorry, must have been a blimblet that went down the wrong way. I should have been more careful." She gazed deeply at Dana as she spoke.

"Jasmine gave me several things for Tremble." Dana turned back and looked straight at Belladonna. "It was like a toy store. I had one full room of all sorts of items. I could have opened a baby shop." Dana paused and smiled. "I will have to go back and think about them. I believe I made a list."

Belladonna shook her head and sat back down. Tremble realized that even though Belladonna's lips never moved, she heard her aunt utter the word 'mortal' in a condescending tone. Tremble's eyes narrowed as Belladonna looked back at her.

"Now that Tremble has turned twenty-one, I think that she should immediately be brought to Neverwrong so that she and I can go find Jasmine together." Belladonna's voice was commanding. Her tone was unemotional.

Tremble thought she could hear CeCe gritting her teeth. She wondered if her senses were now sensitive to her immortal counterparts.

"Your Royal Highness, we have much work yet to do with—" Laken began to answer. Tremble noticed that although his voice was calm and reverent, his stance had a little defiance in it. He seemed on guard.

"We are wasting time. I shall rephrase so that *all* of you will understand me. You shall bring Tremble to Neverwrong within the next forty-eight hours." Belladonna's eyes turned black as coal. She quickly rose and began to walk away.

"NO!" Tremble's reply was not so much loud as it was firm and direct.

Belladonna stopped in her tracks and slowly turned back to face them. She walked back to where she had been sitting and got even closer than before. There was only the illusion that they were in two different worlds. She was so close to Tremble that she could almost feel her breathing.

"Young lady, you shall do as I say. Until my sister and her husband return to rule, if ever, I am the ruler of Neverwrong."

"Excuse me, Belladonna, but with all due respect, that is not correct."

Both Tremble and Belladonna shot Laken looks of shock. Belladonna's look was dripping with anger. Tremble's was amused.

"The Article of Succession as set forth by her Most Royal Highness Queen Jasmine states that in the absence of her and King Forrest, you are the highest ruler of Neverwrong." Belladonna's face broke out in a smile. "Until their heir turns twenty-one." The smile vanished.

"Oh, my goodness, I had forgotten about that." Bridget stood up and walked toward Laken. "All these years, we have been so caught up in making sure Tremble grew up safely, we forgot about that at twenty-one she would not only increase in power in the magical sense, but also in governance."

"This is ridiculous. This child was raised a mortal and is in no way fit to rule our kingdom. She doesn't know the first—"

"You are absolutely right." All heads turned toward Tremble. "She is. I am not fit to rule Neverwrong. I don't know the first thing about it."

"Now, Tremble is showing some wisdom and understanding. You are so much like your mother, dear." Belladonna's tone immediately changed and her smile became bright. "They will bring you to Neverwrong, and I will begin to instruct you in how to rule, and then the two of us will go find—"

"No." Tremble's tone was back being very firm and direct. "You shall continue to rule Neverwrong until my parents come back, and they will, as soon as I find dear Uncle Scordato and we have a nice long chat." Tremble turned and started to leave the room. "Oh, I want the two best male protectors that are outside somewhere to stay, but I want all of the other protectors, except those in this room, sent back to Neverwrong. We will not need their services any longer. I believe that my people here are more than powerful enough to help me find my parents and anything else that I need. Is that good with you guys?"

One by one, Tremble looked at each of them. Laken was the only one who did not give a shocked affirmative nod immediately. After he looked deep into Tremble's eyes, he too nodded in agreement.

"Very well, then. That will be all, Belladonna. You are dismissed. Always a pleasure to speak with you." As Tremble turned and walked away, she snapped her fingers and the screen went black. "Any questions?"

"I am so incredibly proud of you, daughter." Dana tackled Tremble with a huge hug from behind.

"You are walking on dangerous ground, Tremble." CeCe's tone was stern. Her expression revealed her real feelings with the smirk that crossed her face. "I'm with you one hundred percent."

"Ditto, darling. Bridget has your back. CeCe and I know just the two best protectors to pick from the ones currently assigned."

Tremble walked toward Laken. He looked older to her some-how. "Well, what about you? Has all of your training under Bel-ladonna's tutelage made you loyal only to her?"

Laken was silent for a few moments. Then, he slowly knelt down in front of Tremble, took her hand in his, and kissed it.

"I am your humble servant, Princess Tremble."

"I told you before about that princess stuff." Tremble pulled her hand away from his and bopped him on the head. "Get up from there. I do not want you kneeling before me. I want you fighting beside me."

Tremble turned and looked at all of them, individually, and then as a group. She took a deep breath.

"I realize that my defiance of Belladonna is dangerous and, perhaps, willfully reckless. I will not have her dictate how this plays out. All of this has been hidden from me for my whole life." Tremble looked at Dana. "I know that it was as a protec-tion, but the fact remains that I have been living a fantasy in this mortal world. I have loved this fantasy so much. Now, it is time for reality. It is a scary one. I need as much help as I can get. Yet, I feel I only need help from those that I know I can trust. I think that I can trust everyone in this room. Perhaps, I can trust Bel-ladonna as well. I do find it a valuable piece of information that Jasmine did not reveal everything to her, all those years ago or even now. Her message to us was in code. Words that my mother would understand, the one with whom she entrusted her child. I think that is significant."

"Sit down, Tremble." CeCe and Bridget exchanged looks. Bridget began to put up a shield around them. "You too, Laken. What we are about to discuss stays with us."

Laken nodded and sat down next to Tremble. Dana sat on the other side.

"Jasmine, Forrest, and Belladonna were close growing up." CeCe began the story. "As I believe I mentioned before, Anton was a friend of theirs as well. They were childhood playmates and then teens together. What I did not mention is that there was a fifth friend in this group. His name was Xavier."

"Hmm, I've not heard that name before."

"No, Tremble, you have not. And, I would suggest that you don't mention that name outside of this present company." CeCe held up her hand as Tremble began to speak. "I am getting to that. Bridget knew him better than I did, so I will let her explain what he was like."

"Tremble, I know that one of Dana's favorite movies is *Gone with the Wind*, and thus, I know you have seen it several times and are familiar with the characters. Your father, Forrest, is Rhett Butler—charming, debonair, reckless. Jasmine is Melanie—generous, loving, and compassionate. Xavier was Ashley—honorable, chivalrous, and gallant. Belladonna is Scarlett—headstrong, jealous, and relentless."

"Really, I would have cast Jasmine more in the Scarlett role. I mean, she was determined to bring me here and probably defied many people in the process."

"You have seen but one segment of Jasmine's life, one snapshot of her. Albeit, it is no doubt the most important thing she ever did. Yet, this act does not encompass all that she is." Tremble grew silent as she considered CeCe's words.

"Those four were Royals. Xavier descended from the line of Gwenora. He was a very distant cousin to Jasmine and Belladonna, as was Forrest." Bridget tilted her head as if she was remembering. "Xavier was fun loving and good natured. He was athletic and studious. His hair was the color of gold with beautiful white streaks like you would see on a lifeguard in this world. His eyes were emerald green."

"Bridget will go on and on. Xavier was a dreamboat with a personality to match. Everyone loved him, especially Belladonna." CeCe's left eyebrow went up. "Xavier was in love with Jasmine."

"Oh my, this is beginning to sound like a soap opera." Dana spoke up from her corner.

"You keep referring to him in the past tense. Is that intentional?" Tremble was afraid that might be a key element to the story.

"Yes, it is. That is why we are telling you this story."

Bridget stood up and made a screen appear. An image appeared of a very modern looking city. Five young people were sitting around a table with books in front of them.

"This is the Academia of Neverwrong. It is the equivalent of an elite university in this world, such as Harvard or Yale. The five we have mentioned were all students there, as were CeCe and I." Bridget changed the view to show the entire campus.

"Wow! It looks like a college campus in this world, except it is rather futuristic looking."

"Yes, Tremble, very similar. Remember, we have said that this mortal world and Neverwrong are parallel realities. Neverwrong is a little more advanced. You might say it is ahead of time here."

"And, that's because?"

"Mainly, because we send the technology to this world. Our 'great minds' vacation here, especially in their later years. They leave some of their ideas behind."

Tremble studied the view of the campus in front of her. The students were maneuvering from place to place on what looked like skateboards that were hovering a few feet off the ground.

"I've seen those before. Where have I seen them?" Tremble

stood up and moved closer to the screen to point. Before Bridget could answer, Dana spoke.

"Hoverboards. They were in the *Back to the Future* movies. Your father loved them"

"That's it. So was that movie made by—"

"Don't ask." CeCe shook her head. "Just know that they are very real in Neverwrong. They are also newer versions now that are more advanced."

"And use less magic to power." Laken spoke for the first time in the conversation. "You can get a license to use one at the age of twelve. It is a rite of passage kind of thing. I rode one every day to school."

"Let's get back to the story." Bridget took the screen view back to the original scene that showed the five sitting at a table. "As I said, these five were very close and as sometimes happens with friends, some of their feelings began to change as they got older. Tremble, you are right, it was a little like a soap opera or your average college experience, perhaps. Belladonna fell in love with Xavier. Anton fell in love with Belladonna."

"Really?" Laken could not conceal his surprise.

"Xavier fell in love with Jasmine. Forrest and Jasmine only had feelings for each other. There was never any doubt about your parents' love."

"Okay, so there were all of these love triangles. I know that Jasmine ended up with Forrest. What happened to Xavier? Why are you telling me about this?" Tremble looked from Bridget to CeCe and back again. The women had grave looks on their faces.

"Please do not misunderstand us. Belladonna's love for Jasmine is strong and deep. Sisters they are though, and there were times of rivalry. You are right to question our comparison of Jasmine to the character of Melanie, for Jasmine's draw to all those around her is indeed more like what you see of Scarlett. Jasmine's heart is pure nevertheless. She did not see the attraction that Xavier had for her. She was oblivious to his romantic feelings. Forrest saw it clearly as did Belladonna. Jasmine's focus was on healing and helping others. Since your creation, that shifted to your protection." Bridget paused and nodded to CeCe.

"Tremble, as Jasmine grew toward your age, her love for your father grew strong. Xavier's feelings grew as well and he attempted to woo her from Forrest. It caused conflict between him and Forrest, sometimes physical conflict." CeCe stopped and looked at Laken. "Anton often found himself breaking up their battles. As you shall begin to see, magical powers increase exponentially as you reach the age of adulthood. For someone who has always used their powers, the changes can sometimes be subtle and not realized. That was unfortunately the case during the last clash between Xavier and Forrest."

"Oh, no." Dana's words caused Tremble to glance at her mother. "I know what this is about now."

"It was time for them to graduate. They had gone to the Garden of Mystery to have a day of enjoyment. Forrest used that time to announce that he and Jasmine were going to be married. Hurt and frustration rose quickly in Xavier. Anton later told me that it was as if someone had flipped a switch in this young man. His rage grew quickly. In an instant, he aimed a powerful spell at Forrest. Jasmine saw this, ran between it, and repelled it. She had just crossed over into her twenty-first year. She did not realize the power she possessed. As she repelled Xavier's magic, some of hers mixed with it. Jasmine only meant to prevent the spell from hitting Forrest."

"She killed Xavier?" A flash went through Tremble's mind, a powerful light.

"Jasmine accidentally killed him." Bridget shook her head and wiped tears that had fallen. "It was a horrendous accident."

"Jasmine is a healer. Couldn't she reverse it somehow?" Tremble glanced at Dana. The woman was shaking her head. "Did she tell you about this?"

"No, not directly. She just mentioned a great sorrow. I could tell that Jasmine felt deep grief and regret about whatever had happened."

"Jasmine's healing powers are unmatchable. There are rules connected with healing powers though. One of them is that you cannot heal what you yourself have hurt. Jasmine's powers mixed with Xavier's. It was partially her power that killed him."

"Surely Jasmine is not the only healer. Couldn't they have gotten him to someone who could have cared for him?"

"Unfortunately, as I mentioned earlier, they were within the Garden of Mystery. It is a beautiful place. Rare and ancient spells guard it. No one can enter with the intent to harm another. Yet, what goes on within its boundaries is permanent, unyielding. Not only did Forrest announce his marriage to Jasmine there, he had also proposed to her earlier. Anton thought that was what provoked Xavier. He knew the permanence of their love. It was a double blow for his demise. Jasmine's healing could not work and his death could not be reversed."

"Belladonna saw it all. She saw her sister kill her love. This is the same woman who Jasmine entrusted with her kingdom and her child's care."

Tremble stood up and began to pace in front of the window. Bridget had removed the screen and opened the drapes.

"I do not understand."

"Belladonna saw it. Her horror was great. Of course, her blame, at first, went to her sister. Jasmine was at the center of all of it. Xavier loved Jasmine. It was the root of everything. More than anyone though, Belladonna knew her sister's heart. She knew it was an accident. Jasmine left her kingdom in Belladonna's hands. Jasmine knew that a sense of duty would dictate Belladonna's actions. Jasmine left her child in another woman's hands. That, my dear, is why I am cautious of Belladonna. That is why we are about to reveal to you another, lesser known, part of the prophecy."

Chapter Eight

"WE'VE TOLD YOU a great deal about the aspect of the prophecy that reveals what will happen to Neverwrong." CeCe continued the story.

"Yes, the heir will forsake her homeland. I got that part. No pressure there." Tremble smirked.

"There is another part of the prophecy that very few people know. In fact, the only reason that I know about it is that Anton told me. Only very few Royals were told this. Jasmine's mother revealed this piece of information to her daughters, long before anyone ever dreamed that Jasmine might have a child. I do not know if Forrest even knows this."

"Why would part of the prophecy be hidden?"

Tremble was listening so intently to CeCe's words that Laken's question startled her.

"Precisely because of the nature of it. It invokes a great deal of responsibility and a hard choice for the heir to make."

"Welcome to my world." Tremble's sarcastic tone was tinged with a tension that was growing inside her. "Please, tell us. Complicate this story in my mind a little further."

"It is a simple statement. It will not be a simple choice if you choose to fulfill it. 'The heir shall reverse an act of love.'"

"Reverse an act of love? Something that I have done?" Tremble resumed pacing and began to rub her forehead.

"No, Tremble, I do not believe it will be something you have done. This information is the reason that I have concerns about Belladonna—"

"I can no longer sit by and listen to you accuse Her Royal Highness of acts of wrongdoing. She has done nothing—" Laken rose and walked toward CeCe in a confrontational manner.

"You will sit down, young man."

Bridget rose and put her arm out to stop him. He kept moving toward CeCe. Before Tremble realized what was happening, Bridget had cast a spell that put Laken quite forcefully back into his seat.

"We are not accusing Belladonna of anything. We are merely making Tremble aware of some of the history and circumstances revolving around the situations she will encounter. She has a right to know that some may have hidden agendas."

"But, you do not know that Belladonna has such an agenda." Laken did not attempt to move from his seat.

"Yes, we do."

"How?"

"Your father told me. Shortly before his death, Anton told me that Belladonna had spoken to him about the hidden part of the prophecy. She said that perhaps Jasmine's child could reverse the act of love that killed Xavier."

"What? She wants me to bring someone back from the dead?

This is getting way too twisted for me."

"CeCe, this does sound like something that would be dangerous or part of dark magic." Dana got up and joined Tremble in her pacing.

"Dana, I understand your concern, but magic is only dark when there is evil intent attached." Bridget patted Dana on the shoulder as she led her back to her chair.

"Tremble, no one is saying that you should or could bring Xavier back." CeCe resumed speaking. "This is however something that is in the back of Belladonna's mind." She eyed Laken. "I know that it is a desperate attempt to get back someone she loves. It could have serious implications for everyone involved, especially when dealing with Scordato."

"Why is that? What does he have to do with Belladonna?"

"Hopefully, nothing. We do know that he has learned to do some incredible acts of magic. We believe that is why he created the prophecy in the first place."

"Meaning?"

"CeCe means that it is possible that Scordato learned how to manipulate time. Perhaps, he went into the future to see what might happen with his family. He could have created a self-fulfilling prophecy. He could have seen what was going to happen and patterned the prophecy around it."

"It sounds an awful lot like the chicken or the egg dilemma." Tremble noticed that everyone was nodding except Laken. "It's the analogy of which came first, the chicken or the egg. A chicken lays an egg. An egg produces a chicken. Was the prophecy created by someone or did the prophecy create itself?"

Laken scowled and shook his head. "Mortals have such strange philosophies."

"You are afraid that Belladonna is only interested in trying to force me to bring Xavier back? Couldn't there be lots of acts of love that could be reversed?"

"Most certainly there could be. We have no way of knowing what Scordato was predicting. His prophesies are quite vague in many respects. Knowledge and caution are your two strongest allies—knowledge of what you do know and caution regarding what you do not." CeCe walked over to Laken. "Did Belladonna ever mention Xavier to you?"

"No. She actually spoke very little even about Jasmine and Forrest. Most of what I know about them has come from the historical archives or from the memory images of others." Laken stared at CeCe as if he was looking right through her. After a few moments, he spoke again. "She did make one statement to me on several different occasions that she never really explained. She said that when the time was right, I would understand it."

"What was it?" CeCe sat down in a chair next to him.

"She said that I should not blame myself for who I was. That I must accept my destiny."

Tremble watched as CeCe and Bridget exchanged not only a look, but what she was sure was an unspoken message. Bridget caught Tremble's eye before she spoke.

"Belladonna was probably referring to your destiny as Tremble's Protector."

Tremble did not believe that was what Bridget was truly thinking. Bridget caught Tremble's eye again and made an almost undetectable nod of the negative.

"I do not think that is what she meant. I am honored to have that destiny."

Laken did not look at her. He did not see the smile cross her face. No matter what lay hidden regarding him, Tremble knew she could trust Laken. She needed to learn to understand his devotion. She had to learn to have patience with him and to allow him to be her Protector. Tremble could not help but feel that there was more to the story than CeCe or Bridget cared to admit. She was afraid that there was something terribly amiss regarding how Laken entered into the world.

THE MORNING WAS quiet. Everyone went their separate ways and prepared for the day. Tremble returned to her room. About an hour earlier, while they were in the heated discussion downstairs, she had noticed that Choo Choo had headed upstairs. Tremble found her precious pet snuggled in the blankets of her bed. She was chewing on a ribbon that was decorating a small box.

"What have you got there, little girl?" Tremble reached for the box as Choo Choo let out a low growl. "None of that, I think that box must belong to me. It's my birthday." Choo Choo was not about to let go of the ribbon, so Tremble slid it off the box and let the dog have it.

"Mom must have left this here for me to find. Maybe she didn't want the others to see it."

Tremble began to try to open it. The box was made of wood with beautiful carvings of flowers on each side. Glimmering jewels were also inset giving the box an incredible sparkling effect.

"Why is this so hard to open?"

"Because it is enchanted."

Tremble about jumped out of her skin as she turned to find Bridget standing behind her.

"I'm sorry, my dear. I came to check on you and saw that you were opening a present."

"I think it is from Mom, something secret for me."

"It is from your mother, Tremble. Just not the mother you have known all these years. Jasmine has sent this present to you."

"How can you tell?" Tremble looked back down at the box.

"As you grow and learn more about magic and get to know more enchanters, you will begin to recognize that each person's spells have identifying markers or traits. Several things about that box show me it came from Jasmine. One is that I can hear a small whisper of music around it. I think this is because I spent some time with her learning some basic healing spells when we were young. Her spells are very lyrical. In contrast, Forrest's spells were very quiet. Color is a huge factor in identifying them. Your eyes are not trained to see this yet, but I can also see tiny butterflies floating around this box. The butterfly is like Jasmine's signature, it is personal to her, a token of who she is."

"Why is that?" Tremble gazed down at the box and tried to open her mind to be able to see the tiny creatures that Bridget could see. Her hands were shaking with excitement as she wondered what was inside.

"It is because it represents a pure spirit and the process of renewal. The symbolism associated with the butterfly through the ages in all cultures and worlds is vast and diversified. Yet, it all comes back to renewal, hope, and pureness of the soul. The beautiful transformation that this being makes before it flies away. You are making that transformation now. I am certain that is what this gift is all about."

Bridget pointed to the box and smiled. Once again, Tremble tried to open it. None of the sides would budge.

"This is a gift of magic. You must open it with your heart before you can open it with your hands."

Tremble crinkled her brow as she considered Bridget's words. She looked down at the box. Her mind imagined it opening and revealing the contents from within. It remained perfectly still. Tremble looked back at Bridget who was now sitting beside her on the bed. She glanced behind her and saw that Choo Choo had stopped chewing on the ribbon. Her little friend looked up at her with its tail wagging in encouragement. Tremble wondered if her canine companion could sense the magic, if she understood its power.

Taking a deep breath, Tremble began to think about how she wished for the box to open. How even though it was frightening, she was ready for this adventure to begin, ready to learn the secrets—

And, just like that, she began to feel it. Tremble looked down at her hands and saw that the different sides of the box began to move. It looked like a wooden puzzle working itself. One side shifted out, another shifted in. It twisted and turned until it was ready to reveal the contents from deep inside it. A smile took over Tremble's face as a golden light shot up from within the box and thousands of those tiny butterflies that Bridget had just described began to flutter all around.

"I can see them." Tremble looked at Bridget. Her smile shone with love. "They are so beautiful, so tiny, so—"

"So Jasmine. She has come to you on this day. Where she cannot physically be, she has come through magic." Bridget put her arm around Tremble. "Make no mistake. Jasmine's powers are mighty. This act of love caused her great pains to accomplish. Receive it with appreciation."

Tremble looked down at the box. The light grew brighter and brighter, and then suddenly ceased. As if being pulled up by the tiny butterflies, an object rose from within. The glow from it was so blinding that Tremble could not tell what it was.

"The light you see is the magical power that this object contains."

Bridget stopped speaking as CeCe entered the room.

"This is from Jasmine."

"Most certainly. You also can recognize her magic."

"It is so strong. I am amazed at the strength since she has been in seclusion for so long." CeCe drew closer to Tremble. The light was still too blinding for her to see the object held in front of her. "Perhaps, Jasmine's sequestering has allowed for the enchantment to build in intensity."

"She has been saving up for this very special day."

"That's wonderful, but I cannot see what it is. The light is so bright. I need sunglasses."

CeCe and Bridget laughed softly. They both stood in front of Tremble. The object hung between them and her.

"My dear, we cannot see a light. This is part of Jasmine's spell for you and you alone. Relax your mind. Lay your heart's worries aside. Drink in the love that comes with this special gift. There is a message here for you to receive."

Tremble closed her eyes and took a deep cleansing breath. She moved the box from her lap before she opened her eyes again. As she did so, she thought of the woman who had sent her the gift. Jasmine was a stranger to her, yet, she felt Jasmine's spirit all around her. It was comforting. Tremble's mind raced back through time. For a moment, she saw a beautiful woman with raven hair lying in a bed holding a small bundle. Tremble smiled, as she knew she was the bundle. Tears flowed down the woman's face and touched the cheek of the baby. Tremble now felt the tear on her own. To the side, she saw a young version of her mother standing nervously at the foot of the bed. The woman whispered in the baby's ear and kissed the child on the forehead. She placed the bundle in the waiting arms of Dana and the image disappeared.

"We shall meet again on a special day. My love will stay with you until then."

Tremble spoke the words that Jasmine had whispered in her ear. As she opened her eyes, she no longer saw the bright light. In its place hung a necklace, the chain was a twisted rope of yellow, white, and rose gold. It looked delicate and strong at the same time. At the end of the chain, Tremble found a pendant shaped as the profile of a butterfly. It was made of silver and she could tell that there was more to the piece of jewelry than its exterior shell.

CeCe and Bridget drew closer and looked at it. The pendant was hanging in midair by tiny little fluttering friends. Tremble giggled.

"It looks as if they are hovering around the mother ship."

"How observant, Tremble." Bridget's laugh was its normal bubble. Tremble realized that she had not heard Bridget laughing as much in the previous few days.

"Jasmine is a sly one." CeCe smiled as the pendant spun around showing them an identical profile on the other side. "It looks as if it is perched with wings back, ready to fly away."

"This looks like the same piece that—" Bridget stopped speaking mid-sentence. "I believe you should give those tiny friends a rest and take possession of this special gift. I am sure that you have only seen the beginning of what it truly is."

Tremble reached out her hand and the pendant and chain slid into her grasp. The silver metal exterior was shiny and smooth. She noticed that a button clasp joined the two wings in the back. As she turned it over in her hand, she saw that the top and bottom were the same polished silver. Twinkles of color shone through the intricate design of each wing as a swirling design cut into each side like the unique markings of a real butterfly.

"What's going on?"

All three of them jumped as Dana spoke as she entered the room. They looked at each other and laughed.

"Jasmine has sent a gift for Tremble." Bridget stepped out of the way so that Dana could get closer.

"Oh, I didn't hear the doorbell. It must have come while I was in the shower."

Again, the three exchanged glances before bursting into laughter.

"Mom, it didn't come via Federal Express. It was, ah, more like Enchanted Express."

"What is the matter with me?" Dana joined the laughter. "I didn't know there was such a thing."

"Probably because our deliverers do not wear shorts." CeCe's reply sounded dead serious. Her eyes told a different story.

"What do they wear? And how do they get here?" Dana seemed intent on finding out.

"Mom, CeCe is joking. I believe that Jasmine sent this package herself using magic."

"Of course, she did. You, CeCe, are a very bad girl. No fair leading the gullible mortal on."

"Oh, Dana, you are anything but gullible. I think you have too much enchanted birthday cake in your system." CeCe turned back to Tremble. "You appeared just in time. Tremble was about to open this beautiful pendant that Jasmine sent her."

Dana walked closer and looked on as Tremble turned the piece of jewelry from side to side so that her mother could get the full effect.

"It is very detailed and I can see some gorgeous jewels within it." CeCe had kneeled down and was looking at the pendant from below it. "If you open that clasp, I bet it will look like a whole different piece once it is fully opened."

All eyes were on Tremble. She looked at her mother. Dana gave her a wink. Tremble took a deep breath and pushed the button on the clasp. Instantly, the two wings spread and more little tiny butterflies came bursting out from within the pendant. Just as quickly, each one flew back toward the now open pendant and placed a tiny jewel in the wingspan. All of them gasped in awe as quickly the open wings filled with dozens of tiny stones, all glittering in a beautiful multicolored sequence. When the last stone was in place, the butterflies disappeared.

"Oh, it's so gorgeous. Help me put it on."

Dana moved behind Tremble and took the two sides of the long chain in her hands. Tremble thought that she could feel her mother's hands shaking a little as Dana clasped the necklace. Instantly, a swirl of air passed through the room and a voice began to speak.

> *"My darling daughter, how I have dreamed of this day. It has been my strongest hope and desire that you would reach your twenty-first birthday as a happy and healthy, but equally strong, young woman. My confidence in dear Dana and Andrew was not in vain. You have grown up in the most loving environment I could have imagined. I am forever in their debt."*

The voice of Jasmine was like a melody. It reminded Tremble of the musical numbers in the black and white movies that Dana loved so much.

> *"The time has come for you and me to be reunited. It is one of the reasons that I have sent this gift to you. It is not an ordinary necklace. It is a token of return. I cannot physically come to where you are. It is also not safe for me to tell you where I am. Please assure Dana that I am in a safe*

place, unhindered by anyone. Tomorrow, the full power of the token shall come into being. You will begin your journey to me. It will not be a lengthy one. We must make sure that no one follows you. In order to do this, there will be many spells to take you from one location to the next. Laken shall accompany you. He will be the only Protector with you. The two of you shall make this journey. I shall make it possible for you to communicate with the loyal ones who have so selflessly guarded you these many long years. We shall use a bit of mortal technology with a magical twist. Five of these devices shall arrive during this night. One for each of you, including Dana. I know the pain a mother feels when she cannot communicate with her child. I shall not allow Dana to feel that."

Tremble looked at Dana. The woman had a broad smile as tears ran down her face.

"I shall leave you now to enjoy this day of your birth. Rest assured that every day you have been safe has been a day of celebration for me. I give you one last piece of information as a warning. I am in thought communication with Forrest. His life force is still strong. Yet, it is hindered. He cannot confirm what I am about to reveal for fear that Scordato would follow this thought to me. He may be entrapped in the Garden of Stone. It would seem a logical place for Scordato to imprison him. Be aware and travel to me safely, my dear. My heart leaps with excitement at the thought of being able to hold you in my arms again. In closing, I will tell you one last thing. The necklace, the butterfly, was created with the deepest level of magic known to our world. Do not take it off for any reason. It is the life force that shall reunite us. I love you, my darling."

The room became quiet. Holding on to the pendant with her right hand, Tremble began to walk around the room.

"What are you doing?" Dana began following Tremble as she was looking all around the room.

"I don't know. I guess I am checking to see if she is here."

"I can assure you, Tremble, she is not. Her life force is so strong it would be very difficult to hide. That is precisely the reason she sent this package and message on its own." CeCe moved closer to Tremble and began to examine the pendant. "The enchantment around this object is as powerful as I have ever seen. One thing that I imagine Jasmine left to us to advise you about is how to use it. I suggest that you pull the wings down and return it to its original state while you are still in the mortal world. Would you not agree, Bridget?"

"Yes, most definitely. It is a beacon of power in its present state."

"What's going on? Who is doing a summoning spell?"

Before Tremble could comply with CeCe's suggestion, Laken came into the room.

"Oh, my. That has to be from Jasmine." Laken moved closer to Tremble.

"See. It's a beacon." Bridget smiled as she moved out of his way.

"Is this your birthday present? It reminds me of the guardian tokens that The Seven passed down to their firstborn children."

"You are correct, Laken. You have learned the history well. I had forgotten about that." CeCe turned to Tremble. "As Laken said, The Seven each had tokens that they wore throughout most of their physical lives. We do not know how the tokens originated. Each of The Seven passed it to their firstborn at some point. It is thought to be infused with powerful protection spells."

"I am going to head to the kitchen to begin making Tremble's birthday brunch. This morning is almost half over and all we have had was cake. Prepare to enjoy all of your favorites, my dear." Dana commented as she walked toward the door.

"Yes, Laken. Jasmine has sent Tremble a gift for her birthday." CeCe began to explain to him as he examined the pendant. "I had just advised her to return the pendant to its original clasped state so that it would not draw the attention that you are now giving it."

"Is this what Tremble will use to find her? Will it map the journey?"

"Again, you are correct. Your powers of discernment have increased today as well."

"I have prepared my whole life for this journey, remember?"

"Indeed. We have not forgotten. Jasmine has bestowed this token on her daughter. Jasmine has said that Tremble's journey will begin tomorrow and that you will be the only one to accompany her. Bridget and I will be meeting with you shortly to further prepare you for this responsibility. Your role as The Protector of the heir of Neverwrong is about to begin."

Laken released his grasp on the pendant. He gazed into Tremble's eyes with such intensity that it made her a little uncomfortable, yet, something kept her gaze equally as strong as his until he looked away.

"I am ready. I shall give my life if necessary to protect you."

Laken turned to CeCe and Bridget. His posture was of a soldier going off to war. The image made Tremble's mind wander to Jake. She had seen a text from him flashing on her phone when she first arrived in her room. She wondered if he was now on his way across the world. Like her, he was taking a dangerous journey filled with the unknown. Where he would go would not be his choice, he would honor his duty. It was something they now shared.

"Tremble, we shall leave you to get ready to enjoy this day." Bridget gave Tremble a brief hug. "Hide the wings of that beautiful butterfly."

"Oh, I had forgotten." Tremble quickly closed the wings

back on the pendant. She felt a little shift in the air around here. The room felt normal again.

"Yes. That is better." Bridget followed CeCe and Laken out of the room. She turned back as she reached the doorway. "Make the most of this day. I am not going to say that it is your last day in the mortal world. I do not believe that is true. After you have ventured into our magical kingdoms, this life shall pale a little in comparison. You will not love it any less. This is your home, your roots, and always will be. I am afraid that it will not be the same though, no matter what you encounter in the days and weeks to come."

Bridget closed the door behind her and Tremble sat back down on her bed. Choo Choo had taken the ribbon and settled into a chair in the corner of the room. The small poodle now jumped back up onto the bed and nuzzled Tremble's hand for some petting.

"It looks like I am going to have to go on a trip tomorrow, Choo. I really wish I could take you with me." Tremble felt the vibration of her phone on the bed. Picking it up, she saw that she had many phone messages and texts. Several of the texts were from friends at college. Two were from VeVette. Scrolling back further, the first one of the day had come Jake. It was simple—"I love you to another world and back." Tremble choked back the tears that instantly came. She had forgotten about how he had always told her that he loved her to the moon and back.

"I guess Neverwrong is about as far away to Jake as the moon is."

A feeling of fear and anxiety came over her. It was a wave of emotion. As quickly as it came, it also began to leave her.

"Maybe some of Forrest is in me, too. Perhaps, he has sent me a little of the warrior gene for the days ahead."

Tremble stood up and walked toward her closet. Most of her clothes were at her apartment. She began to wonder what she should do about her other home.

"You don't have many clothes here for this time of year."

Tremble about jumped into the closet as her mother spoke.

"I'm sorry, sweetheart. I thought you might have heard me come in. I did not mean to scare you. I just wanted to check on you. It's been an emotional morning."

The grey in Dana's hair was more than she usually allowed. Yet, Tremble was amazed at how youthful her mother continued to look despite all of the circumstances life had dealt her.

"I was just thinking about my apartment. What do you think I should do about it?"

"Do about it? Nothing. I will continue to send the rent check and get your mail for your other bills." Dana turned Tremble around to face her. "You are going on a journey to another world. That is scary for you. It is horrendously frightening for me, too. I have no doubt about one thing—you will be coming home. To this home, the mortal home that you were raised in. What you decide to do after you take care of Scordato is a whole other discussion. Maybe you will summer in Neverwrong." Dana's southern accent on the word 'summer' made Tremble smile.

"How can you be so sure that I will come back? Everything that we have learned about Scordato indicates great power and great evil."

"Jasmine. She is the reason I know you will return. I know in my heart that she thinks you can defeat him. You can make right all that he has wronged. If she did not believe that, she would not be summoning you. There is plenty of danger, no doubt. I trust Jasmine more than I fear Scordato. You should, too. She's made some wise decisions so far."

"Oh, yes, indeed she has. She gave me to you."

THE REST OF THE day was about all things that Tremble loved. After listening to all of her messages and getting dressed, she went downtowns to find a dining room table filled with all of the brunch foods she loved. Tremble gorged herself on her mother's wonderful cooking; ignoring the calories she normally counted.

In the afternoon, she and Dana slipped away to an old downtown theater in a neighboring town. Tremble's birthday happened to fall on a Sunday and the theater showed classic movies. A Jimmy Stewart marathon was showing that afternoon. They wandered in as Mr. Smith was making his historic journey to Washington.

"I want Jimmy Stewart to go with me to Neverwrong." Tremble announced as she threw her empty popcorn bag in the trash.

"Having him along would be better than any magic spell." Dana threw her candy box away and the rest of her soda. "We ate too much junk."

"Absolutely. I have no idea where we put it after that brunch. How did you cook so much so quickly?" Tremble was so full that her eyes hurt.

"I had a little help."

"Ah, Bridget Child, no doubt." They both laughed.

"Yes, she is very handy in the kitchen. Most of her cooking spells involve her winking at pots and pans, I've discovered."

"Winking?"

"Yes, this morning, she would read a recipe, say a few words, and then wink at the container I wanted it in. It was interesting to watch."

Tremble and Dana walked down the street toward where they had left their car. There was more activity than Tremble realized. They soon understood why as a band was setting up on the lawn of the courthouse.

"I'd forgotten about the Jazz festival they hold here."

"Your father loved it. We used to come every year."

"I remember."

Tremble's memory flashed back to a similar evening in her teens. Her parents were sitting in lawn chairs near where her mother and she now stood. She remembered a man walking toward her with a very fat poodle.

"I had forgotten that this is where we met Choo Choo's mother."

"Oh, yes, she was so big with puppies that her belly was dragging the ground."

Tremble stopped on the sidewalk as the memory of that day became even clearer.

"What was the name of the man who we got Choo Choo from?" The man's face was suddenly clear in her mind. She recognized the face.

"Oh, his name. Give me a minute. It was unusual." Dana stopped a few feet ahead of Tremble and turned back. "It was Scordato, Mr. Scordato." The realization of what she had just said became apparent on Dana's face. "Oh, surely it wasn't."

"Oh, yes, it was."

"BEFORE I TELL YOU this, I am going to make something perfectly clear." Tremble looked around the table. When she and Dana had returned home from the movies, Tremble had asked the others to meet them in the dining room. "Nothing, I mean absolutely nothing happens to Choo Choo."

"Tremble, I fail to see what your dog has to do with anything that we have been—"

"Laken, stop talking and listen. We got my dog from Scordato."

"No, that's impossible." CeCe stood up from the table and made a screen appear behind where Tremble was sitting. "I'm certain that one of your guardians was with Andrew when he went to purchase Choo Choo."

Time seemed to whirl back faster than Tremble could digest it. The screen was a blur. The movement was so fast that it almost made her sick.

"I'm sorry. I cannot focus on the right time slot. I am finding before and after Andrew's meeting with the owner of the dogs. I'm not finding the precise point of the transaction."

Tremble noticed that for the first time that she could ever remember, CeCe looked like she was coming unglued. The look on her face was frantic.

"Calm down. Look at the evening of the Jazz Festival. He had Choo Choo's mother on a leash." CeCe nodded and resumed looking. A few seconds later, the scene popped up on the screen. A younger Tremble was on the ground petting a very pregnant poodle. Dana was talking to a group of women seated nearby. Andrew was standing, talking to the man who was holding the dog leash. It was Scordato.

"Does he look like Scordato to you? He looks nothing like him to me. Are you sure you are not mistaken?" CeCe's look had downgraded from frantic to anxious.

"He looks exactly like him, just like the Scordato we saw in the scene with his siblings after he had transformed himself from the emaciated rags look. This man looks like he stepped off a movie screen. Do you remember him, Mom?"

"I vaguely remember him, but like the others, what I see on the screen is not the same image that we saw of him earlier."

"He's worked a spell to protect his identity, no doubt." Laken spoke up. "A spell that works on everyone but Tremble. CeCe, I think it is as has been speculated about her. She may be immune to the spells he can cast because of her heritage from two lines of The Seven."

"None of this discussion is addressing the root of all of this. What is the significance of Choo Choo in this equation?" As Bridget spoke, Tremble clutched her furry friend tighter.

"I'm not going to say this again. Nothing happens to Choo Choo."

"Now it's time for you to calm down." CeCe smiled as she petted the dog's head. "Whatever purpose Scordato had in giving you Choo Choo, he's had years to use it. It hasn't caused you any harm, so what can we do?"

"Perhaps, it was one of his silly games to prove that he could infiltrate our guard of her." Bridget casually waved her hand and the scene that CeCe had created disappeared.

"How did you do that? That was CeCe's spell."

"CeCe and I have worked together for so long that it is like being married. I can finish her sentences, too." Bridget smiled briefly. "Tremble, I think the message here is clear. Scordato has been watching you, all your life."

In a flash, everything moved. All five of them were within what appeared to be a cyclone. Just as quickly, the feeling ceased and they were sitting around a table in a plain white room.

"What just happened?" Tremble's arms were empty. "Where's Choo Choo?"

"I left her in the dining room. She will be fine. We are actually still there as well." Bridget showed them an image of the room. Everyone appeared to be sitting around the dining room table talking. "We needed privacy. It is now obvious that Scordato or some of his minions have been monitoring your life. Perhaps, your pet is one of the means by which he does that. Perhaps not. Either way, it will not hurt for us to have a conversation without Choo Choo in the room."

"Where are we?" Dana was holding the edge of the chair she was sitting in as if she would fly away.

"We are in an enchanted room." CeCe leaned over and reached for Dana's hand. "There is nothing to fear. We are not very far from your dining room. Bridget could not give you a warning of what was about to happen. An illusion has been created to hide what we are really doing."

"Tremble, this may be the last time that we can speak to you in this guarded manner. It will considerably drain our magic for us to hold this enchantment together for the time we need. We must convey to you what you need to know about the devices that Jasmine is sending."

"If Scordato is monitoring us, doesn't he know about those devices?"

"That is very doubtful. I am sure that Jasmine protected that entire conversation under its own special enchantment."

"CeCe is right. I tried to get into your room during that time. I could not. It all made sense to me later." Laken spoke up.

"As we are doing now, I'm sure that Jasmine created some sort of decoy to protect that time."

"She did. I saw it. Everyone was in the living room during the same time I couldn't get into Tremble's room." All eyes went to Laken. "I thought it was just a girls' thing and you didn't want me around as I tried talking to you, but no one would answer me."

"You weren't in the illusion?" CeCe tilted her head as if she was studying Laken's reaction.

"No."

"Perhaps, Jasmine also created a diversion spell so that no one would see themselves if they came upon the illusion." Bridget answered the question that CeCe seemed to be ready to ask.

"She's a sly one. I have missed her so."

"Okay, back to this illusion." Dana had loosened her grasp on the chair but did not appear to be any more comfortable with the situation.

"Yes. We need to explain these devices. They will look like cell phones, only more advanced than any this world has yet to experience. They are powered by magic and will allow you to communicate with us, and only us."

On the table in front of CeCe a device that closely resembled a cell phone appeared. It was the size of a checkbook. With a wave of her hand, it began to grow in size until it almost filled the table.

"Dad would have loved this, from cell phone to sixty-inch screen in the blink of an eye." Tremble exchanged a smile with Dana.

"There shall probably not be many times when you will need the screen to have this function. It will be useful if you wish to enter a scene you are viewing through the screen." Bridget's tone was very matter-of-fact.

"Hold on. You've lost me." Laken spoke up. "I've never seen this level of Neverwrong technology. I don't understand what you just said."

"This is top-secret technology. It is what Forrest and his

associates were working on at the time of Tremble's birth. It was mainly created to be used during confrontations with other warring kingdoms or in surveillance efforts." CeCe's answer was direct. "It is exactly as Bridget has said. The magic that governs this device would allow you to view a situation on the screen and enter that scene. It must be in the present or future time."

"Future time? This is a time travel device?" Tremble grasped her head in her hands.

"Only in the present or future, you cannot go back in time and change anything or interact with the past."

"But you can change something in the future?"

"Yes, it is not advisable though. Only in situations that are dire and disastrous."

"Couldn't this entire situation be described that way?" Dana's look of fear had changed to worry. Tremble noticed that the youth she had seen earlier had left her mother's face.

"We must keep in close contact with you. You must allow us to advise you when it might be prudent to use this device. It will be what shall map your way to Jasmine."

"I thought my pendant was going to do that."

"It shall be a piece in the puzzle as well. The pendant will tell you when your next piece of instruction shall be coming."

As if on cue, Tremble felt a vibration and saw that a beautiful purple glow was coming from within the pendant's clasped wings.

"Open it." Laken's voice showed his excitement.

Tremble opened the clasp and the beautiful multicolor-jeweled butterfly came into view. Instantly, a device appeared in front of each of them. The image on the screen was of the same butterfly.

"Oh, my, that is amazing." Laken's eyes grew big, as he

reached out to pick up his device.

"It is fantabulous!" Tremble could see that her aura became visible and quickly changed into several colors before reverting to her personal purple shade. "There is something very reassuring about this. Maybe it is because, for the first time, this is in terminology that I understand. Because of my father, I understand technology and its power. I can see how this will lead Laken and me to Jasmine." Tremble paused and caught Dana's eye. "For the first time, I am not afraid. I do not really begin to understand magic. I know that I will, in time. I *get* this magical GPS. We're going on a trip and this butterfly will be our guide."

Laken stood up beside her with the device in his hand. Tremble joined him. Immediately, their devices synchronized and Jasmine's face replaced the image of the butterfly.

"Thank you, CeCe and Bridget, for making this protected communication possible. It makes my heart happy to see the smiles of determination that I see on the faces of Tremble and Laken. Tomorrow morning, your first instructions shall appear. CeCe is already aware of your first destination. Please know that while this device has the most advanced technology that Forrest's team has been able to develop, it is possible that it will fail us during your quest. In the event that this happens, Tremble and Laken, you must call upon your instincts and your own inner strengths to direct you further. I shall be patiently waiting."

There was silence for a moment. Jasmine looked as if she had something else to say.

"Dear Dana, it is wonderful to see your face. I wish that I could embrace you again. My simple words will not adequately convey the depth of my gratitude to you and to Andrew. My heart has been heavy with grief these past few years for you and Tremble in the loss of him. I promise that I will do everything in my power to keep our girl safe as she makes this journey to me and to her destiny. I have every confidence that she will be able to right the wrong that was put into play long before her birth."

Jasmine paused again and looked behind her. When she turned back to them, Tremble noticed that the smile had left her face.

"I will conclude this conversation now. We must be careful. Even under the protection of CeCe and Bridget's advanced powers, our communication could be monitored. My dear Tremble, I look forward to your arrival. If at any point you feel threatened, turn back. Laken, I am counting on you to help her make that decision, if needed. My love shall blaze a path ahead of you."

The image of the butterfly returned to the screen. Everyone was silent for a few moments before CeCe spoke.

"We will take the two of you to the airport in the morning. Your flight leaves before dawn."

"We're flying to Neverwrong on an airplane?"

"No, you are flying to New York City on an airplane." Bridget answered as she tried to get past the butterfly image and into the tablet-like device.

"Jasmine is in New York?" Tremble looked confused.

"No, but New York is the first destination on your journey. All of the major cities in the United States have portals to Neverwrong. Remember though, Jasmine may not be in our homeland. It would have been dangerous for her there."

"If I am the one who can fulfill the prophecy, why is it dangerous for Jasmine or Forrest?"

"That's a very good question and I wish it had a simple and logical answer. Unfortunately, it does not bode well for your extended family or the neighboring kingdoms." CeCe shook her head. "Before I answer, we can leave this protected state. Let's remember though that we cannot discuss your impending departure."

They all nodded. With the waving of both CeCe and Bridget's arms, they were all back sitting around the dining room table. Choo Choo jumped up into Tremble's lap.

"The details of the prophecies were kept secret for decades. As information has a tendency to do, it eventually became more common knowledge." CeCe looked tired as she began to answer Tremble's question. "The first generation or two that descended from The Seven were very protective and reverent about the information. As the distance between The Seven and their heirs grew, there was a little less loyalty in the ranks. Everyone thought that the best way to avoid the fulfillment of the prophecy was for none of the lines to unite, so the heirs sought marriage in our neighboring kingdoms, among the commoners of Neverwrong, or in this mortal world."

"Although Jasmine and Forrest were greatly loved by the family, for the most part, there were those who were fervently against their marriage, even to the point of violence. That was only amplified when Jasmine became pregnant." Bridget continued the story. Tremble noticed that she looked pale. "It is the main reason that she came to this world so early in her pregnancy. She was afraid of those who might try to do her harm."

"Harm, in what way?" Dana spoke from within the kitchen where she was preparing iced tea.

"There were those who said that Jasmine might have some sort of accident that would cause her to lose her child." CeCe took a deep breath and shook her head. "Others talked of developing a spell to terminate the pregnancy. These threats were taken very seriously."

"For the most part, the impending Royal birth was met with

happiness. Even though there was a high chance that this heir would be the fulfillment of the prophecy, some felt that it was also time for that to occur and whatever happened would be as it should be."

"So, if Jasmine isn't somewhere in Neverwrong, do you think she is in the immortal world?" Tremble nodded as her mother set a full glass in front of her.

"There are arguments both ways for and against that idea." Laken took a sip of the beverage and made an unhappy face. "It would actually have been easier for her to remain hidden in this world."

"I have just got to say something." Tremble took a drink of the tea. She made the same face that Laken had. "CeCe and Bridget, you two don't look so good."

"We are fine. Just a little tired. It's been a long day." CeCe winked and Tremble remembered that they could not talk about where they had just been.

"Maybe a little food would do us good." Bridget winked also as she stood up and followed Dana back into the kitchen. "Laken, I think that I am remembering that one of your favorite dinners is Alfredo."

"Oh, yes." Laken visibly perked up.

"And, that you love seafood."

"Right again. Crab, especially."

"Precisely what I was thinking." Bridget paused and looked at Tremble. "Would you agree, my dear, that it would only be appropriate for us to honor Laken with his favorite dinner?"

"I think that is a wonderful idea. Especially since, I also love the items that were just mentioned. I love everything about today, except this tea." Tremble set an almost sleeping Choo Choo down on the floor as she rose and carried the rest of her glass of tea back to the kitchen.

"Oh, no, is there something wrong with my tea? You love my tea." Dana took the glass from Tremble. First, she smelled the liquid then she tasted it. "It tastes fine to me."

"I agree with Tremble. I have drunk your tea for several weeks now and have loved it. It is that classic Southern sweet tea that everyone talks about."

"Now that you say that, nothing has really tasted right today. Even that popcorn we had at the movies was a little off. I hope that Laken and I aren't getting sick."

"You two are not sick. It's sort of a coming of age thing." Bridget spoke up from the kitchen. Tremble could see that she was also chanting and winking.

"Bridget's right. As your powers change, your taste buds do, too. Bridget can fix that as she is creating dinner."

"Well, I'm glad that it isn't my tea." Dana smiled as she picked up a full salad bowl from in front of Bridget.

They all gathered in the kitchen and watched Bridget "cook." It reminded Tremble of an artist creating with clay. She seemed to be creating beautiful works of food from nothing. The aromas were intoxicating.

Dana and Tremble slipped away to freshen up while Bridget was finishing. As they walked up the stairs, Dana looped her arm through Tremble's.

"I'm going to miss you. It's like you are going off to college all over again."

The emotion of the day seemed to have hit Dana. She was crying. Tremble pulled her into a hug.

"I'll come home on weekends." Tremble whispered the words she had said when she had left for college three years earlier. This departure was hardly the same. "I promise." It was all that she could say.

"Tremble's cake was impressive. My cake is out of this world."

"Well, your cake wasn't from this world either."

Dinner with all of Laken's favorites was finished and Bridget had just made Laken's cake appear. The cake did not make its entrance all in one piece. Instead, the different layers flew in and landed, one on top of the other, like a spaceship landing on a planet.

"Wow, Laken. I hope that cake tastes as exciting as it looks." Tremble ducked as one of the layers flew dangerously close to her head. "Watch it, Bridget."

"Nothing like a little excitement. Laken, each of the layers has one of your favorite flavors. It's a mixture of this world and your homeland, so Dana and Tremble; you might want to taste all of them."

The last layer reached the top and the entire cake exploded. Every color imaginable burst forth all around them. Tremble glanced at her mother as a concerned look crossed Dana's face as cake flew everywhere. When the show was finished, in a blink of an eye, the cake was back in one piece and seemed to be swaying a little.

"Oh, now, I really like that part." Dana smiled as she saw that not even a speck of icing was visible anywhere except on the cake.

"We know as a child, Laken, you were obsessed with all those space movies from this world. We thought that a compilation of them would be appropriate for your cake."

"I am so impressed. It's like a sci-fi marathon that you can eat."

No sooner had the words left his mouth than a large plate appeared and began to receive small pieces from each of the cake's ten layers. Each layer was a different color and flavor.

"No, butterflies and foo foo for the Protector of the heir to Neverwrong." Bridget giggled. "That just would not do at all."

After the cake event was over, presents appeared. Tremble was amazed at the variety of presents that CeCe and Bridget gave Laken, including some that she simply did not understand. She was equally amazed that her mother had managed to purchase some gifts for him. Tremble laughed as he pulled a long pair of lounge pants out of a box.

"No Superman on those, Laken." Tremble laughed as she saw that the pants were a solid black with a silver stripe going down the outer side of each leg. Another similar pair in grey with matching shirts was also included. "Hey, you've got one more present on the table. See?"

Tremble pointed to a small black box that was barely visible under a mountain of crinkled wrapping paper.

"There's no card. Which one of you got me this?"

CeCe and Bridget exchanged looks before their gaze shifted to Dana. All three women shook their heads at each other. All eyes shifted to Tremble.

"I wish I did have a gift for you, Laken. My shopping time has been minimal."

A concerned look crossed CeCe's face. Laken looked at her as he started to open the lid.

"Be careful."

A bright, silver light was instantly visible as Laken slowly opened the box. From Tremble's seat, she could see that the box contained a large round disc of some sort. Laken peered closely at it, and then turned the box toward CeCe who was now standing over him.

"It's a pendant with the seal of the Royal Force of Neverwrong Protectors. There are only a few of these in existence."

CeCe took the pendant out of the box and turned it over in her hand. Tremble saw a long chain fall through CeCe's fingers as she examined it.

"Where would it have come from?" Laken looked from CeCe to Bridget for an answer.

"I don't know. The only time I have ever seen one of these is in the museum at headquarters. They are very rare."

"My father didn't have one?"

"No, Anton did not. When he passed, we were given an Honor Medal for his service." CeCe turned to Dana. "It is sort of like a Purple Heart in this world. It is given for heroic service." CeCe again directed her attention to Laken. "That medal is safely stored in a vault for you. Anton did not have one of these. This is very old and probably encased in magic."

"Let's find out." Bridget took the pendant out of CeCe's hand and set it down on the table.

"You look like you are about to do something dangerous."

"She is, Dana. Don't be afraid, Bridget specialized in spell breaking in her early years with the Bureau."

Bridget began whispering and waving her hands over the medal.

"She is trying to get it to communicate with her."

"Talk to her? How is that possible?" Tremble's look of confusion made CeCe laugh.

"No, Tremble, not in the conventional sense of the word. Bridget can communicate with the power that might be within it and possibly find out where it came from."

"Loquere libere."

Bridget said the phrase a couple of times before causing magic to come out of her own fingertips. Instantly, a force pushed back at her, causing the woman to fall on the ground.

"It doesn't want to talk to me." Bridget nodded her gratitude as Laken helped her up.

"What were you saying to it?"

"Loquere libere is speak freely in Latin." Dana's reply was quick.

"Yes, that is correct."

"You speak Latin in Neverwrong?"

"Dana, we learn the languages of the entire world. Our realities are parallel. Our influences are as well. Latin is one of the most ancient languages. It has greatly been influenced by the magic world, and vice versa."

"This medal is cloaked in powerful magic. I can only surmise that it is for your protection. I cannot imagine how it would have fallen into the hands of evil." CeCe picked up the medal and handed it back to Laken. "We could contact Belladonna and see if she knows anything about it. I do not think it came from her, though. She would have told you that herself."

"I agree. There's something telling me that we should keep this information to ourselves, at least for now."

Laken took the pendant and put the chain around his neck. As he did so, a deep green glow emitted from it. Laken did not seem to notice it. Everyone else darted their eyes at each other in acknowledgement of what they saw. The worry lines on CeCe's forehead grew deeper. In a few seconds, the glow disappeared.

No one said a word about it. Tremble knew she should not forget what she saw.

"I'M SORRY, MY darling, but you are going to have to put up with me and Choo Choo tonight." After everyone had gone, Dana appeared at Tremble's doorway, clutching her own pillow, a box of cheese crackers, and two bottles of water.

Tremble smiled at the familiar sight. All through her childhood, anytime that Andrew would go out of town, Dana would appear in Tremble's room with the same items.

"Who's afraid tonight?" Tremble laughed as her mother climbed into her big bed. Choo Choo quickly moved to the foot of it and dug herself a comfortable hole in the covers.

"As it always was, it is me. I'm afraid."

Dana made a pouty-like child's face as she positioned her pillow among the many already behind her. Tremble watched as she pulled one of the smaller ones out and threw it on the floor. Dana's process was much like Choo Choo's in obtaining the perfect position.

"Yes, you were afraid. I had to protect you while Dad was away."

"Yes, and you still are. Choo Choo and I will be sleeping right here while you are gone."

Dana handed Tremble one of the bottles of water and opened her own. She leaned down over the side of the bed and poured some water in Choo Choo's waiting bowl. The canine companion jumped off the bed to check it out. She lapped a few drinks, and then jumped back on the bed to begin positioning the covers again.

"Crackers in bed, huh?"

"It's tradition. One thing that your father and I did not agree on."

"I remember. Eating any type of food in bed was an abomination to Dad. He used to tell me that I would find mice in my bed if I ate in it."

"I know. One of the few serious fights that your father and I ever had was about him telling you that. You came to me crying the next morning because you dreamed there were mice crawling all over you. I will never forget what you said to me about it, it was so sweet."

"What did I say?"

"You said that the mice weren't the friendly kind, like in *Cinderella*."

"Gus and Bruno! I loved them. Oh my, I don't remember telling you that."

"Why should you? You were only four. That is why your father and I fought. It was a horrible fear to put into a little girl's head."

"You have to admit though compared to the real fears you all faced protecting me, mice in my bed was a little tame."

"Well, I suppose." Dana scowled as she opened the box of crackers. "It still was not the right thing to do."

"So that's why you started coming to my bed when he was out of town. Now, that I think about it, you always brought food."

"Exactly. I wanted to prove to you that nothing horrid would happen if there were crumbs in your bed. Besides, even when he told you that, Hershey would have taken care of those unfriendly mice."

"Oh, Hershey, my whiskered friend. I loved him so."

Choo Choo's ears perked up at the mention of the name.

"Don't worry, Choo, he's long gone." Dana held out a cracker to Choo Choo. The dog sniffed it before taking it out of Dana's hand.

"I guess it was a good thing that Hershey was an older cat by the time we got Choo."

"Definitely, they did not like each other for one second." Dana paused and thought for a moment before chuckling under her breath. "I guess you don't know where we got Hershey."

"No, he was always around for as far back as I can remember."

"He belonged to Jasmine. After we came home from the hospital, he was here. It was one of the reasons I knew that Jasmine was truly gone."

"Wow. I never knew that. I guess that wasn't something you would have told me." Tremble paused and thought about the big fluffy Persian cat. "Did Jasmine name Hershey?"

"Yes, Jasmine loved chocolate. She told me that his coloring reminded her of a Hershey bar. Some things are universal with pregnant women and eating chocolate is one of them. He was a grouchy ball of fur after this one arrived." Dana handed Choo Choo another cracker.

"You know, Mom, I wonder if the reason that Hershey and Choo Choo didn't like each other was because of where they originated?"

"What do you mean?" Dana mumbled through a mouthful of crackers.

"We have just realized that Scordato had something to do with us getting Choo and now you have told me that Hershey came from Jasmine."

"Oh, my goodness. You are right. I can't imagine what it all means."

"I don't want to imagine what it all means. Choo Choo has been the best dog ever." Tremble reached down and scratched her apricot-colored friend behind the ears causing the canine to flip over on her back and wait for belly scratches. Tremble obliged.

"Yes, maybe we are putting too much stock in who they came from instead of remembering how much a part of our family they have been." Dana offered more crackers to Tremble before closing up the box. "I am so sleepy. Your birthday took a lot out of me."

"Me, too. I'd brush my teeth again, but the bathroom seems too far away."

They both broke out in giggles as they scooted down under the covers.

"I was thinking the very same thing."

Tremble turned off the lamp beside her bed. Her eyes were drawn to the full moon that shone through her window.

"I wonder if Neverwrong has a moon as beautiful as that."

"From what CeCe and Bridget say, it is the same moon. It's probably a different color though."

"Oh, I don't understand all that. How can we be in parallel realities and some things are still so different?" Tremble let out a big sigh. "You've got to promise me something, okay?"

"Sure, my darling, what?"

"Promise me that if you and Choo sleep in here each night while I am gone, you will look toward the moon like we are right now. On the nights that you can see it, please talk to me."

Dana moved closer to Tremble and pulled her into a hug.

"I'll do better than that. I will talk to you every night. You've got to promise me one thing as well."

"Anything."

"You have to remember that you really can't trust anyone completely, except Jasmine. Laken, Belladonna, even CeCe and

Bridget, all seem to have your best interests at heart, yet we are not sure who else might be influencing them."

"You saw the green, too. It's not the first time."

"I know. It may mean nothing, and he does not appear to have any knowledge of it when it happens. You still need to be careful. Put your full and unconditional trust only in Jasmine."

Dana kissed Tremble on the forehead and pulled her even closer as the two of them closed their eyes to sleep.

Chapter Nine

THE HOUSE WAS quiet when Tremble rose. As she tried not to disturb her mother, she noticed that her alarm clock was blinking. Choo Choo was nowhere in sight.

All the bedroom doors were closed as she walked down the hallway. When she reached the downstairs, Tremble pulled out the cell phone she had slipped into her pocket.

"Three o'clock. No wonder no one is up yet." CeCe had told her that they would leave at five in the morning to head to the airport. "I could get some more sleep."

"Hello. Tremble, is that you?"

Tremble rubbed her eyes and looked around to see who was talking.

"Tremble, this is Belladonna. Please come speak with me if you are there."

Tremble froze as she saw that there was a light coming from behind the living room drapes. She took a deep breath and thought about what she should do.

"Go ahead."

Laken whispered from behind her. Tremble almost jumped over the couch.

"Don't do that!" Tremble whispered sternly and hit him on the arm.

"I'm sorry. I heard you get up and I followed you."

"Tremble, dear, please talk to me." They heard Belladonna's voice again.

"I think you should talk to her. I will stand back where she can't see me."

Tremble stared at him for a moment, and he nodded again. As she walked toward the window, she stubbed her toe.

"Ouch!"

Tremble pulled back the drapes while still hopping on one foot.

"Hello, Belladonna."

"Hello, Tremble. Are you okay?"

"Yes, I stubbed my toe as I was walking over here. What do you want to talk about?"

She hobbled back to sit on the couch in front of the window. She saw Laken move toward a far corner of the room near the doorway to the stairs. It was out of Belladonna's viewing area.

"Is someone else there with you? I heard you talking to someone."

As if on cue, Choo Choo jumped up on the couch beside Tremble.

"I was talking to my dog. I just got up to get a drink of water. I'd like to go back to bed."

"Certainly, I realize that the hour is late. I will be brief." Belladonna paused and looked down. As she raised her head again,

Tremble noticed that her aunt looked very nervous. "I want to apologize for my behavior. I have been very stern and controlling. It was not my intent. It worries me that you are going to search for Jasmine without having the proper protection."

Belladonna paused and looked intently at her. Tremble remained silent.

"I wanted to talk to you again. You must understand; I only have your best interests at heart. It would be more prudent for me to know your whereabouts and for part of our legion of protectors to be with you at all times."

"Thanks, but I think that Laken and I will be fine on our own."

Tremble watched as the color changed in Belladonna's face. Her jaw tightened. It almost looked as if she were aging. Her skin seemed tighter when she clinched her teeth and her nostrils flared slightly.

"No, you will not. You will not be fine with Laken. You do not understand."

A very sick feeling came over Tremble. It reminded her of the time that she had vertigo. The world seemed to tilt and the bile of nausea came up in her throat.

"What do you mean? He was created to be my protector, the Protector. As I understand, it was under your care that this occurred. I should be safer with him than anyone."

Tremble could almost feel Laken's presence behind her. She could hear him breathing.

"Yes, he was."

"Is there something you want to tell me about that, Belladonna? Did you do something wrong?"

Tremble now realized there were some things that even magic could not conceal. She watched as Belladonna's aura changed into many different colors before settling into a silvery gray tone. She had not learned what the colors meant, if there were meanings. Yet, Tremble could understand that Belladonna must have been warring within herself.

Belladonna adjusted her clothing and improved her posture before she answered Tremble's question. She also took hold of the red diamond pendant and gently stroked the stone.

"My actions are not on trial. Laken was under my supervision and care. His heart is pure and resolute in his duties to the Kingdom of Neverwrong."

"Then, why are we having this conversation in the middle of the night?"

"I think it is foolish for you to refuse the help that is rightfully yours." Belladonna's eyes narrowed. She stared straight ahead at Tremble. It took everything inside of Tremble to not lean back from the gaze. It was like looking into the eyes of a snake that was about to strike. "You cannot carry out your mission if you are not alive to do so."

"I have no fears of death before I meet Scordato."

"You are such a foolish child." Belladonna rose from her chair and turned to walk away. The abrupt action made her long silver dressing gown twirl.

"Scordato will protect me."

"What?" Belladonna turned back and faced Tremble.

"Scordato will protect me." As she spoke the words, everything became clear to Tremble. "He has been protecting me all along. Perhaps, even more than my guardians have."

"You have come of age and lost your mind. Now, I must insist that you have extra protection. I may need to travel with you myself—"

"She's right." From the shadows of the room, Laken appeared. "Tremble is right. Scordato has been protecting her. I know this is true."

"How long have you been there? You should have made your presence known to me."

"Laken is under my direction now. Make no mistake, Aunt Belladonna. Remember, I AM the heir of Neverwrong."

Tremble did not know how, but she felt Laken squeeze her hand. Looking down, he was not touching her. Again, Belladonna twirled to leave the room.

"I will tell my dear sister that I tried to save you from yourself. I will tell her that you foolishly thought you were being saved by the very one who prophesied about you."

"Scordato will not allow me to come to harm until the prophecy is completely fulfilled. It would make him wrong if anything happened otherwise. I'm sure he does not want to be wrong."

Belladonna had moved farther away while Tremble spoke. She now stopped in her tracks. She did not turn around.

"What do you know of Scordato or the evil that came before him?"

"I know a great deal." Laken spoke before Tremble could answer. "That is why I am her Protector. I shall give my life to protect hers."

Still, Belladonna did not turn around. It made Tremble wonder what she was trying to conceal from them.

"I will be awaiting your cries for help. We will hope that our legions can get to you quickly enough. I shall wash my hands of the responsibility." Belladonna finally turned back toward them. She was further away and the light was dim. It was hard for Tremble to see her clearly. "Just like Jasmine you are. You think you can fix everything. You cannot."

Belladonna clapped her hands and the screen disappeared.

"You're right about Scordato. I do not know why that had not occurred to me. He wants you safe until the time that he can challenge you himself. He wants to battle you like he would have battled Baldric."

"Everything just clicked in my mind. I think that he is the one who keeps the evil at bay as well."

"Yes, that would make sense. He knows the evil because he has part of it within him."

"From what happened in the Garden of Stone when he touched his mother?"

"Precisely. Baldric saw that something happened to his brother there. It may truly have been the reason why he consciously or subconsciously allowed Amadeus to be considered dead." Laken paused as Tremble turned to start to leave the room. "Do you think there is something wrong with me?"

"You mean what Belladonna was saying?"

"Yes. I do not know what to think of that. She seemed to be warning you about. She groomed me to protect you. It was always all about you."

"Laken, I am not going to call Belladonna's motives into question at this point. It is futile, and we do not have time. My instincts do tell me that she may not be all that she seems. She may have more of an agenda than protecting her sister's daughter and the Kingdom of Neverwrong."

"Does it make you distrustful of me because of my connection to her? What if I have been somehow subconsciously programmed to cause you harm?"

Tremble gave Laken a long serious look. Seeing him in his new pajamas minus the superhero characters made him look even more like one of the young men she knew in college. They were dying to be men, yet they were really still little boys in many regards.

"Laken, I trust you. I cannot say that has always been the case. It is how I feel now. I believe that in your heart you are loyal to me. Whatever happens, we will face it together."

"I am glad to hear that. I hope I can live up to your expectations"

"We better go back to bed and see if we can salvage a tiny bit more sleep. Who knows when we will get to do that again?"

"LADIES AND GENTLEMEN, welcome aboard US Airways Flight 2064 with non-stop travel to New York. This is Aretta Covington, your chief flight attendant. On behalf of Captain Keith Barrett and the entire crew, we welcome you. Our flight time will be—"

"I've never flown on one of these types of flights before."

Laken flipped through the emergency instructions pamphlet while Tremble looked out the window. CeCe had dropped them off at the airport ninety minutes earlier. The goodbye with her mother had been the hardest thing she had done since Tremble said goodbye to her father.

"What do you mean? Haven't you flown before?" Tremble smiled as a young flight attendant walked by eyeing Laken.

"A flight in this world." Laken looked up and gave the attendant an awkward smile. The young woman moved along. "Why was she standing there staring at me?" Laken whispered to Tremble. "Can she tell I've never flown before?"

"I don't think so. From the look on her face, she finds you attractive. There will probably be something wrong with my food unless I let her know we are not an item." Tremble stood up a little and looked around. The attendant had walked from first class to the coach class area behind them.

"I really haven't studied mortal dating habits. I didn't think I would need to know about them."

"Can they be that different from the world you grew up in?" Tremble leaned closer. "I would refrain from using the m-word while we are out in this world."

"Okay, I understand. We need to be incognito."

"Yeah, that." Tremble laughed to herself. "Oh, Miss, excuse me." The attendant had almost zoomed by them. Luckily, she had given Laken a glance that gave Tremble just enough time to get her attention.

"Yes, do you two need something?" The young woman did not look at Tremble.

"Yes, I just wanted to make sure that you knew that my brother is allergic to peanuts." Laken shot Tremble a confused look. "I realize this is a short flight, but I wanted to make sure you knew that. Neither one of us need any. He is deathly allergic."

"Oh, your *brother* has a peanut allergy." This time, the attendant looked directly at Tremble and gave her a big smile. "Thank you very much for letting me know that. We would not want to do anything that would jeopardize his health or the enjoyment of the flight. We have some lovely alternative snacks."

"Thank you, Karen." Tremble stretched to see the attendant's nametag.

Karen gave them a toothpaste commercial smile and turned to head back to the front. Tremble noticed that she had a little more swing in her step. Unfortunately, for Karen, it was wasted on Laken. He was deep into reading the inflight magazine.

"Too bad this isn't a longer flight. We would have just scored huge shrimp cocktails."

"Oh, I'm not allergic to shellfish." Laken gave Tremble a smirk as he put his earbuds in to listen to music.

"Certainly not. Peanuts are a cheap snack. We are in first class, the snacks should be much better than that."

Laken shook his head and went back to reading. Tremble was grateful for the solitude as it gave her a chance to think. Her mind drifted back to how tightly her mother had hugged her just a couple of hours earlier. Tremble knew that Dana had put up a serious somber front when CeCe had told them it would be best for her and Laken to walk into the airport alone with no long goodbyes. Dana had taken a big breath as she held her at arms' length for one last long look. Then, the bear hug had begun and Tremble was not sure if her mother was going to let go. It brought a tear to her eye to think about it. She would try to hold on to the feeling of her mother's hug for as long as her memory would allow.

TREMBLE FINGERED HER butterfly pendant. Ever since the plane had touched the ground, she had felt a tiny little twitch coming from it. She wondered if it was a warning message to alert her for future instruction.

"Well, I have to say that was very easy. The flight was a piece of cake." Laken smiled. Coincidentally, Karen walked by right at that moment and stopped in her tracks.

"Did you enjoy the flight?" She was obviously on a mission to get something done, but the young woman paused at their row for a moment.

"Yes, it was great. I can't wait to get off this plane." Karen's expression instantly changed and she moved on down the aisle.

"You have just ruined her day."

"What? What did I say? I said the flight was great."

"It's going to take a lot more training for you to ever be able to date in the mortal world." Tremble laughed as she unbuckled her seat belt and collected her bag.

"What makes you think I want to do that?"

Tremble paused and watched as Laken retrieved the items they had stored in the overhead compartment. She had not thought about what he would want in regards to his personal life. She only thought about his life in connection with hers.

As they left the plane and crossed the jet bridge into the airline terminal, Tremble's pendant started twitching under her shirt. The action brought her back to the reality of why they were making the journey.

"I think we may be getting some instructions."

Tremble glanced at Laken while entering the huge airport. In every direction, people were hurrying with bags wheeling behind them.

"CeCe told me that you should go into a restroom and open your necklace. I will be able to inconspicuously look at what you see with my tablet since they are synched."

"Okay. That makes sense. I'm glad we don't have any checked bags to retrieve." Tremble spotted the nearest restroom. Not far away was a coffee shop. "Why don't you wait over there and get us a couple of coffees?"

Laken nodded and headed toward the coffee shop as Tremble ducked into the bathroom. A long line of stalls stood in front of her. She chose the one in the farthest corner. As busy as the terminal area had been, the bathroom was relatively vacant.

Once inside, Tremble quickly took out her tablet and pulled the chain from under her shirt. The pendant was glowing in purple. She released the wings of the butterfly and its beautiful image was visible on the pendant and on the tablet screen. Tremble expected to see Jasmine's face appear, instead there was just a swirling image and a very simple message.

"Tomorrow you will have eggs at 555 Met."

Tremble furrowed her brow as she looked at the message. She searched her mind for what it could mean. Shortly, the screen turned black and turned itself off. As Tremble closed the wings of the pendant, her mind swirled with possibilities. None of them made any sense. She had the same look on her face as she exited the bathroom and walked toward Laken. His look did not reflect hers.

"That will be fun." Laken smiled at her as he reached for the croissant in front of him. His tablet lay closed in front of him.

"Fun? What will be fun?"

"Going to the Metropolitan Museum of Art."

"How did you get that out of that cryptic message?" Tremble stood next to him in awe.

"That, my dear Tremble, is why I am your Protector." Laken's grin was broad as he took a bite of the large pastry.

"Is that a chocolate croissant?" Tremble's mouth began to salivate as she saw chocolate oozing out from where he had taken a bite.

"It most certainly is. If you will please back away from mine, you will find one of your own in that bag next to your coffee."

Tremble felt slightly self-conscious as she set down her bags and jumped up on the tall chair next to him. She had not noticed the identical cup and bag at her own place at the table. Skipping the coffee, she dove right into the bag's contents and took an unladylike bite.

"Oh, my. That is just heaven."

"Yes, I am an expert code breaker and pastry selector." Laken took a sip of his coffee before continuing. "One of the things that I was drilled on extensively during my training was identifying special places in this world's major cities. When someone from Neverwrong comes to this world, they usually begin their time in a well-populated area."

"Why is that?" Tremble took a small bite after her first sip of coffee.

"It's easier to not be noticed. There's a certain something about our people that makes us stand out." Laken looked around to the tables next to them.

"Oh, what, like your model good looks? That could have gotten us some delicious first class extras if our flight would have been longer. Karen would have been more than happy to treat you like royalty." Tremble winked as she took another bite of the pastry. "Mom used to make these. They were my dad's favorite. I had forgotten how luscious they could be."

"I suppose that is one of the reasons why several who have come here have become famous. People sense something special about them. It's more the power they possess than their physical attributes."

"Your power of code deduction and pastry choosing is impressive." Tremble wiped her mouth with a napkin, before crumbling it up in the bag. "How did you really figure that out so quickly?"

"You must have some extra powers of perception yourself." Laken raised his eyebrows as he drank the rest of his coffee. "I put 'met' and '555' in a Google search. The Metropolitan Museum of Art's website was the first thing that came up with the information that 555 was one of the galleries there. It currently is exhibiting a rare private collection of Fabergé eggs."

"Sneaky is your superpower, my friend. Or should I say smart?"

"We have the Internet in Neverwrong, yours and ours. Search engines are a wonderful thing." Laken collected their trash and put it in a nearby receptacle. "Let's take this discussion elsewhere. We are in the biggest city in the United States. Let's go check into a hotel and experience some of it."

"It is the day after our birthdays. Where shall we stay?"

"We have Belladonna's credit card. Actually, we have our own credit cards connected to her bank account. According to my research, an establishment called The Ritz Carlton would be a nice location. It is near the famous park."

"Yes, Central Park. I would refrain from calling it the famous one. That will brand you as a tourist."

Tremble and Laken began to walk toward an area where they could get a taxi. She was glad that their luggage was light as they walked down the long corridor.

"What's wrong with being a tourist?"

"Nothing, except that just about everyone in this country has heard of Central Park and they don't call it the famous one."

"Whatever, let's just get through this airport and get a taxi downtown." Laken picked up the pace of his walking. Tremble tried to keep up.

"Don't you think we should have a reservation?" She almost had to yell at him, he was getting so far in front of her.

"I've already made one." He slowed down so that she could catch up.

"When?"

"While we were waiting for our flight this morning."

Tremble decided that Laken was going to be one-step ahead of her in every way he could be.

"WOW. I HAVE STAYED in some beautiful hotels during medical convention trips with my parents, but this is magnificent." Tremble stood at one of windows that viewed Central Park. "I feel like a princess."

"That is an appropriate feeling for you to have. You should get used to it. Trust me, this suite pales in comparison to the Royal Palaces of Neverwrong. You will live very well there."

"I don't know how comfortable I would be with that. I like the cozy feeling of a home. A palace doesn't sound very homey."

Tremble could not stop staring at the view. It had been several years since she had last visited New York City with her parents. She remembered though that a view that included trees was a rarity in the city of skyscrapers. She better understood why the property surrounding Central Park was so prized. Just looking at it made you feel like you could breathe better and provided a level of relaxation that she doubted would exist in many parts of the city.

"You certainly did a wonderful job of selecting a place for us to stay. I'm curious though, why did you give us an alias and use the same last name?"

"For one thing, I don't have a last name, and we are supposed to be incognito, remember?"

"How can you not have a last name? Isn't that confusing?"

"Why would it be confusing? I'm Laken."

Tremble watched as he stretched out onto the luxurious couch in the living room of the suite.

"Couldn't you be confused with other Lakens?"

"There are no other Lakens."

"Oh, surely, in all the Kingdom of Neverwrong there is at least one other person named Laken."

"No, it's not allowed. Duplicate naming is against the law."

"Really? No one ever names a baby after their grandfather?"

"No, each offspring born since the beginning of Neverwrong history has had a different name."

"So you can't even use a name again after someone dies?"

"No duplicate naming, period. It really makes it much simpler."

"Is that rule throughout the entire magical world?"

"No, there could be another Laken in another kingdom. That person's name would have his kingdom at the end. Such as, I am Laken of Neverwrong. It would be rare for that extra geographical add-on to be used. It does sometimes occur for sporting events and news reports."

"Well, that is interesting. You still haven't told me why you picked the name you did for our last name for this reservation."

"I don't know many last names. I have seen that name so many times over the last few weeks in your father's music collection; I guess it was just the first one that came to mind. What's wrong with it?"

"Oh, there is nothing wrong with the name. I am sure they are a fine family. We just will not be incognito being The Presleys. Especially, since we are staying in the most expensive suite in this hotel."

"I thought it was a common, well-known name."

"Well-known? Absolutely. Common? Not so much. Is that the name that is on our credit cards?"

"Yes."

"Oh, this should really be interesting." Tremble sat down in a chair opposite Laken. "That pastry was delicious, now I am really starving. Why don't we go exploring and get some lunch?"

"Sounds like a great idea to me. Then, we can come back and get ready for our night on the town."

"Night on the town? Where are we going?"

"Broadway, where else?"

"Oh, you really are set on doing the New York experience."

"If this has to be a stop on this journey, we might as well enjoy it."

"You and I are going to get along just fine."

LAKEN WANTED TO have a subway experience. He soon grew tired of that mode of transportation and the two of them took a taxi when the distances were too long for walking. It was an afternoon of adventure. They bought lunch from food truck vendors, explored interesting shops, and just took in the sights and sounds of the bustling atmosphere. They decided to have a late dinner after the show they were seeing, so the last stop of the afternoon was an ice cream parlor that Tremble had seen featured in several movies.

"We will need to walk back to the hotel if we consume these sundaes. I do not think I have ever eaten hot fudge that was so delicious." A big glass dish was in front of Tremble that reminded her of a margarita glass. There were three different flavors of creamy ice cream topped with lush chocolate fudge, whipped cream, and nuts. "This dessert is so simple and yet so decadent. Would you be embarrassed if I licked the bowl?"

Laken's eyes got big as saucers as he looked at Tremble mid-bite. She started cackling with laughter. Laken had big eyes and a spoon in his mouth. Tremble laughed so hard that she started hiccupping and the combined sound made everyone around them look their way.

"You can lick your bowl now. Everyone is looking anyway." Laken winked as he joked with her. Tremble was beginning to understand why Karen had been so interested. He did have a certain charm.

Tremble drank some water and tried to calm the hiccupping. After a few moments, Laken finished his sundae and asked the waitress for the check.

"Can you do that thing that CeCe could do that made everyone around us not know what we are talking about?" Tremble leaned into the table and whispered. Laken leaned in as well.

"I already have."

"Oh, so what are people hearing us talk about?"

"Mostly the weather and how different it is than where we live."

"Where do we live?"

"England."

"The Presleys from England. How ironic."

"I don't understand."

"No, I don't believe you could." Tremble took a long drink from her glass of water. "Why do you think that Jasmine chose a museum as our next destination?"

"I was wondering when you were going to ask that. You understand that this world and Neverwrong are parallel realities."

"I understand that I have heard that term several times now. I am still not sure that I understand exactly what it means."

"Perhaps it shall make more sense once you have experienced it. Until then, let me give you an example of one of the aspects of both worlds that are similar on all levels. It is the arts—music, literary, paintings, all sorts of creative endeavors.

The creative world is magical—it is all one. There is magic in every note of music, in every syllable of the written word, in every piece of physical art created with the mind and soul of an artist. In this world and in our world, the magic that is weaved into these things are all the same."

"That I can understand."

"So, a museum of art is a place of magic. It is actually magical hallowed ground, so to speak. It is a great place for a portal. As I mentioned before, Gallery 555 currently houses an exhibit of Fabergé eggs. They are enchantment personified. Their beauty and delicate design are awe-inspiring to all those in the mortal and immortal worlds. Such an exhibit would be an ideal place to portal into another dimension."

"That's the most exciting thing I've heard today." Tremble looked down at the empty bowl in front of her. "It's not the most exciting thing I have eaten, but—"

"Let's go. We need to walk a few blocks before we catch a cab. You are too high on sugar."

They walked in silence, glancing in shop windows as they passed, watching people scurrying around them. Tremble thought about the visit to the museum the following day. The possibility that within twenty-four hours she might be in another world. Neverwrong was getting closer.

"It will take me a week to get that gravity song out of my head."

After short naps and showers, Tremble and Laken had dressed in some of the new clothes they had purchased during their afternoon excursion. A taxi ride to Times Square gave Laken his first glimpse of Broadway. Tremble was not sure if he had intentionally chosen the play they saw because of its magical connection, but *Wicked* had provided a night of enchanting entertainment and one of the play's featured songs had become an earworm for Laken.

"It should be a song that you have no trouble understanding."

Tremble smiled as she looked around the small restaurant they had chosen for their late dinner. The concierge at the hotel had said it was one of the best-kept secrets in the city.

"I'm not following what you mean."

"The song is about defying gravity. You know a thing or two about that."

"Very funny and now you have again reinforced those words in my head." Laken paused and took a drink of water. "We must be prepared when we go to the museum in the morning."

"Prepared for what?"

"Prepared to not return to the hotel. I have a strong feeling that we will not just be viewing the exhibit."

"So, will we check out before we leave?"

"No, I do not think so. I have told CeCe where we are. She can check us out, if needed. We may just disappear."

"Disappear. That is not normally something that people try to do."

"Tremble, no matter how normal and fun our day has been we can't forget that what we are doing is anything but normal. This mission is best defined as unusual in both our worlds."

"Like a movie. I am living a movie."

"Perhaps. That is a good analogy. I do not believe the ending has been written yet though."

"Oh, I am sure that Scordato would disagree with you. Everything we are doing must be part of his prophecy, a part of his plan."

Tremble looked up as the older waitress served them steaming hot plates of pasta. She imagined perhaps that the entrees were created with old world recipes handed down in the woman's family. Tremble knew it was that kind of place.

"I'm sure he thinks that fate must bow to his bidding. He may not realize that fate has its own agenda. Even if, as has been speculated, he made a trip to the future to learn the story time would tell then, it does not mean that time could not have been rewritten since." Tremble stopped eating and gave Laken a confused look. "You could travel a hundred years in the future and experience a certain day. You would think that you knew exactly how it would be. Between now and a hundred years from now though, a multitude of things could have changed the outcome that you would expect. That day could have as many changes as the days that will pass until then. The future is an ever changing being."

"That is so deep and wise, Laken. It's as if you have lived many lives."

"It is a kind thing for you to say, but I do not know that I can take credit. I have read that we carry the experiences of our ancestors in our genes. Unfortunately, I do not completely know who I am carrying." Laken bowed his head and moved his fork through his food.

"You are concerned about what Belladonna said last night, aren't you?"

"I cannot help but be concerned. No one seems to know the entirety of my identity. I fear that there is something evil lurking within me that may rear its ugly head. I shall do everything in my power to overthrow it, no matter the personal cost."

Laken looked so troubled that it caused Tremble to reach out and grasp his hand. He looked from his hand to her eyes. She saw true fear followed by tender thanks.

"I have to admit that I had my doubts about you in the beginning. And, I still have not forgiven you for the influence you cast over Jake." Tremble let go of his hand and leaned back in her chair. "I cannot, however, imagine being on this journey with anyone else. We share the reality of our forced destinies. I trust you with my life."

"I will give my life to protect you. No matter who the enemy might be, I shall not hesitate to make the sacrifice." Laken paused as the server returned to fill their beverage glasses. "I regret what I did to Jake. It was youthful jealousy for the most part. My level of protection was taken too far." Tremble raised her eyebrows and gave him a smirk. "He is a lucky man to have your love. Maybe, someday I shall be on the receiving end of such love."

Tremble paused to realize what she had never before considered about Laken. He was created for specific purposes. His existence was not the plan of two parents who wanted a child. The parents who had raised him were actors in a story created as a means to an end. They had no doubt grown to care for him. Yet, it was not the same as being welcomed into a family and being the center of their love. His youth had been full of training and discipline. Now his young adulthood would be shadowed with danger. He would not even have the college experience that Tremble had so enjoyed. His life was held ransom by a prophecy he was not even in.

Chapter Ten

"**H**AVE YOU EVER **been here before?**"

Tremble and Laken stood at the bottom of the massive concrete steps of the Metropolitan Museum of Art. Looking at the size of the building gave visitors a taste of the extensiveness of what was within. The steps themselves were as much a meeting place as the structure was a home of its priceless contents.

"I have a feeling that I have stood here before."

Tremble looked at all of the people going in and out. Even in the early morning, there were several small groups of two or more sitting on the steps chatting. As she gazed up at the pairs of tall columns that framed the entranceway, her mind drifted back to her childhood. She saw her small foot in a sandal with a flower adorning the top. One by one, she climbed the steps. Each hand held tightly and as her gaze continued up, she saw her young parents on either side of her.

"Yes, I was here with my parents when I was small. It was a long time ago."

Tremble's mind kept showing her that image. Even when she felt Laken's hand on her arm, she could not break herself away from that instant trip back in time. Her heart longed to go back to those days. They were some of the happiest times in her childhood.

"Are you okay?"

Laken's question brought Tremble back to reality.

"I'm fine. I was just remembering. Let's hurry in. It looks like a storm is about to hit."

"Yes, those clouds are looking very dark and grim."

Once they entered the main entrance off Fifth Avenue, they acquired a map and began to orient themselves to the massive structure. It did not take them long to discover that Gallery 555 was on the first floor in the rear of the building. They decided to gradually make their way to the location and view some of the other exhibits along the way.

"Are we really interested in seeing all of these exhibits or are we both just stalling?"

Laken's comment caused Tremble to laugh as she had been having the same thought herself.

"I love art. I'm also terrified to go into that gallery."

"I always find that looking at paintings in this world is very strange." Laken came up from behind Tremble and took her hand as she was looking at a painting by Rembrandt from the 1600s.

"What do you mean?" Tremble realized that she needed to get used to having physical contact with Laken. She had no idea how they might have to help each other. Holding her hand might be a minor action later.

"In Neverwrong, the paintings are animated. The artist uses magic to make the subjects come to life. They move around the painting. The same is true with a sculpture. It has the ability to move and take a new shape."

"I saw that with the portraits of The Seven. I assumed that the ability pertained only to them because of the curse. It never occurred to me that paintings in general could do that."

"You will love it. The colors are breathtaking. Everything in a painting is so alive, because it is, in a sense."

They had begun to walk as Laken was describing the art of Neverwrong to Tremble. Now, they found themselves at the entrance to Gallery 555. There did not appear to be anyone in the room.

"Okay, let's go."

Tremble took a deep breath and entered the room in front of Laken. There were several elevated pedestals under low light. Each contained a beautifully crafted egg.

"I believe I now understand why this room was chosen."

Laken paused in front of the first display area. Within the glass cube was a breathtaking Fabergé egg that was predominantly a rich regal green with intricate detailing all in gold.

"That is just unbelievable. The photos I have seen in books do not begin to do the detail justice. I cannot even imagine how long it must have taken to make one."

"My rudimentary research on the topic suggested that it took teams of highly skilled craftsmen a year to make each design. The designs are so intricate and delicate; I imagine that error was a problem."

"I guess that is why they are so valuable."

"Yes. That and the rarity of the original eggs. A Russian jeweler, Peter Carl Fabergé, and his crafters created them over a thirty-year timeframe from the late nineteenth to early twentieth century. Only sixty-five eggs were produced, fifty of them were imperial eggs for the Russian Royal family."

"Is that why you think we are here, because my ancestors are a royal family?"

"That could be part of it. I was thinking more about the similarity of these eggs to the Neverwrong Royal Butterflies."

"What? Is that why my necklace is a butterfly? Is it a royal symbol?"

"Yes, very much so." Laken looked around. "I'm going to briefly put an invisibility shield around us so that I can show you something."

Tremble watched as with a few quiet words and the flick of his wrist Laken made a cylinder of light surround them. Just as quickly, he created a small screen in front of them. It appeared as if it was a museum setting, much like where they stood. As the view became clear, Tremble saw butterflies—hundreds of butterflies. These were not the real variety like those with her birthday cake. These butterflies were pieces of art. As Laken had said, the art was animated and it came alive before her in ways she could not have imagined.

"I know that you will enjoy seeing this collection in its entirety sometime, but that would take more time than I think we presently have. So, I am going to show you the specific pieces I believe that are our connection with what we have viewed today."

A long glass case appeared, just as any museum would use. There was something different about it though. It appeared to have a level of movement to it. The glass shimmered. There were tiny waves in it that reminded Tremble of the ocean. Amazingly, the movement did not obstruct the view of what was inside.

"These are the globes that are the home bases for the Neverwrong Royal Butterflies. There are eight of them, one for each of Marcellus' and Claudia's children. The globes and their matching pendants were created by a very powerful and creative enchantress who came with Marcellus and Claudia to our world as the nanny for the children. Her name was Inezia."

On the screen appeared a very small woman all dressed in blue. Her right hand was palm up. Within it was a beautiful jeweled butterfly so real looking that Tremble expected it to flutter its wings and fly. No sooner had the thought passed through her head, then that is what the butterfly did.

"Oh, my."

"Yes, indeed. Inezia created these beautiful pieces of jewelry and an intricate glass globe, one for each of the children who were in her care."

"Is she still in Neverwrong?"

"Sadly, no. She disappeared on the same day that Marcellus and Claudia became stone. She went out in search of them ahead of Baldric and Amadeus. She was never found."

"So much loss for those children to experience all at once."

"It made them all become that much closer, especially the sisters. From then on, they were all very protective of each other. Many of them lived together even after they were married. Multiple families in one castle." Laken paused as they watched the butterfly land back in Inezia's hand. "Seven of these globes, each unique, are on display in the Royal Museum."

"Where is the eighth one? I would have imagined that The Seven would have taken Amadeus' butterfly globe with them when they left the mountain."

"They probably would have if they could have. Interestingly, Inezia had it with her when she disappeared. My personal theory is that the evil one took the butterfly and used it to influence

Amadeus. Each butterfly had a spell that linked it to its owner. I think this is why Amadeus turned into Scordato."

"Every story leads back to him, doesn't it?"

"I can see why you would think so. The Royal Family of Neverwrong has a sad and complicated story. I think I have shown you enough so that you can understand why I have correlated the Fabergé Eggs with the Neverwrong Butterflies."

Tremble nodded. With a snap of Laken's fingers, the screen, and the shield around them disappeared. Tremble watched Laken to see what he would do next. He appeared to be doing the same with her.

"Let's just look around at the exhibit and perhaps something will be revealed to us." Laken smiled and held out his arm for Tremble to lead the way.

As Tremble walked around the room, she noticed there were several cases to hold the intricate eggs. Each was a masterpiece. In the far corner, an unusually shaped case was on a triangle pedestal. It was slightly higher than the rest. As she got closer, Tremble's pendant began to vibrate.

"Laken, I think this is it."

Laken came up behind her with his tablet in hand. It was then Tremble realized that not only was the egg a beautiful shade of purple, it also had a very special design on it. The design was a butterfly.

"Give me a second."

Tremble watched as Laken again shielded them from view. This time, it looked like he put a stronger field around them.

"It looks different because I want it to last a little longer. After a certain period of time, it will dissipate." Tremble gave him a puzzled look. "We might not come back this way. Actually, it would only work if we returned together. That may not be."

Tremble paused and thought about Laken's words. Here they were. This was truly the door to the beginning of the journey. She had no doubt that with the next step, she would, for the first time, be in the magic world—the world of the immortals. Tremble was terrified and beyond excited at the same time.

"Are you ready?"

Laken's eyes locked with Tremble's. She shook her head and took hold of the pendant. The glow of color had reached a deep and vibrant shade. It was pulsating with life. Tremble unclasped the wings and the beauty of them came to life. Simultaneously, the same image appeared on the tablet in Laken's hands. Tremble could feel her own tablet vibrating in her backpack. She wondered if Dana's was doing the same. She hoped that her mother could experience the journey with her, in some way.

The screen image changed from the beautiful butterfly to the kind face of the woman that Tremble had just seen moments before. "It's time for you to meet your heritage." The message was brief. The screen went dark. Laken grabbed Tremble's hand and the journey began.

"Laken, I can't see you. Are you still there?"

Tremble felt as if she was falling. Her body was weightless. The speed of travel was such that it felt to her as if she was being sucked down a wind tunnel.

"Yes, I am here. I still have hold of your hand."

"Oh, yes, I feel that. It's so confusing not being able to see anything."

"Just be calm. There is nothing to fear from what we are experiencing now. This is how we pass from one dimension to the next. Albeit, a slowed down version. I am not sure if this transition is happening so that you can understand it better or if it is because we are travelling back in time. I have not experienced time travel. I've only learned about it."

"Why would we be going back in time? I don't understand."

"I don't know, Tremble. If that is what is occurring, there must be an important reason."

Tremble's mind raced as fast as her body was moving. She was surprised that the process of movement was not painful. It continued to feel like one very long fall. Suddenly, she began to see a growing multicolored light from below. She felt Laken's grip tighten around her hand. Her feet touched something firm and the feeling of falling ceased.

While his grip did not loosen, Tremble could feel Laken moving away from her. She had not realized that she closed her eyes when her feet hit the ground. As she slowly opened them, Tremble took a deep breath. She almost let out a gasp as she realized where they were.

"Laken, is this where I think it is?" Tremble's voice was barely above a whisper.

"It most definitely is. You do not have to whisper. I believe we have been transported back in time. I do not believe we will be interacting with anyone. It will be as it was when we were viewing the memories of others, only now we are physically here."

Tremble's eyes began to take in the room that she had already seen many times as she learned about her family. The Library was the central location for the Royal Family to congregate. It held the core of all things that had transpired in the family.

As she looked around, Tremble took a deep breath and smelled the aroma of a fire. The sounds of its crackle lead her eyes to one of the room's corners. The fireplace was huge with a mantle that was about six feet high. This was a portion of the room that she had not remembered seeing before.

"Laken, does this mean that we are in Neverwrong?"

Still holding her hand, Laken drew closer to her. He was not looking at her though; he seemed intently focused on something on the other side of the room.

"Yes and no. The Library is within in the mountain. Technically, it is on the outskirts of Neverwrong. We are, however, now in the magical world. That is why we crossed over into this dimension. We are not in our own time though."

"How can you tell what time period we are in?"

"I cannot tell that exactly. I do not know how to explain it. My magical radar is not picking up any other mortal beings. That is what tells me we are in another time."

Tremble looked down at her necklace. It was no longer glowing. She decided to leave it in its open position for a while. For the first time since this had all begun, she let go of Laken's hand. The movement caused him to look at her as she was reaching for the tablet in his other hand.

"The screen has gone blank. Do you know why it was Inezia on it before? Why would she be involved in this journey? I thought she no longer existed."

As her eyes began fully to adjust to where they now stood, Tremble began to realize that they were not alone.

"I do not know. I guess that is part of what we are here to find out." Laken retrieved his tablet from Tremble and put it in his own backpack. "I'm sure there is a specific reason that we have been transported to this particular place and time. I think we should just stand back and see what happens."

Tremble nodded as they both moved to a vacant area of the room. There were only two people in the room—children—a boy and a girl.

"I believe that this might be Amadeus and Abelia, based on the ages they look."

The boy was sitting on a seat that was part of a bookshelf. He was deep into a book. The girl was sitting quite a few feet away. She looked less casual than the boy and appeared to be doing some form of needlework.

"Children, come in here and take a seat."

A very regal looking man entered the room followed by three girls and a boy. A beautiful woman followed them with a baby in her arm and a toddler holding her hand. The final person to enter the room was Inezia. She was carrying a large wooden box.

"You must all pay very close attention. Our dear Inezia has a very special gift for each of you. This gift is not a toy, although you might want it to be. It is a beautiful and rare present that you must keep with you when you journey outside of our home."

The man was mesmerizing. He had the charisma of a movie star from the glory days of Hollywood. There was no doubt that he was Baldric's father. Tremble could see the resemblance instantly.

Marcellus stepped away and motioned for Inezia to come forward. The woman was petite in stature. Barely five feet in height, if that. Her body structure was small, compact, yet, she looked to have a physical strength that was beyond her size. Her sandy brown hair sat atop her head in a bun. It was the woman's eyes that Tremble found most intriguing. She motioned to Laken to come toward her. He nodded and they moved to a get a closer view as Inezia began speaking.

"Children, your father's words are true and wise. You must heed them." Inezia looked at each of the eager faces who were watching her intently. "My love for you has spilled forth into the creation of something enchanted. It will be your guardian and protector throughout life's journey." Tremble felt a nudge from Laken. "It is not a toy. Just as it shall protect you, you must protect it and make sure that it is always with you when you venture beyond these walls."

As Inezia placed the box she had brought on a table in the center of the room, Tremble and Laken drew closer to her. Tremble became close enough that she could have reached out and touched the woman. It startled her when Inezia turned and seemed to be looking Tremble right in the eyes.

"Don't move and don't say a word. You cannot cross time. It is very dangerous."

Laken's quick words of admonition stopped Tremble in her tracks. It did give her the chance to look deeply into Inezia's eyes and see that they were a beautiful shade of purple, unlike any that she had ever seen before. With specks of gold within, they looked like magic themselves.

"Come to me children."

Inezia looked away from Tremble. Laken pulled her away from the spot where she was standing.

"Don't get that close again. You were within the reach of her power."

"I don't understand. I thought—"

"Don't question, just heed. I cannot explain it now. You were in a very dangerous spot. I wouldn't have been able to protect you there."

Tremble nodded and moved to the other side of Laken. He was now a buffer between her and everyone else in the room.

"Bring the youngest to me first."

Claudia took hold of the toddler's hand. The baby was still in her arms. They walked toward Inezia.

"That would be Elsavetta and Verina. I have talked with them about this very moment. Neither of them has any memory of it."

"You've talked with them?" Tremble gave Laken a shocked look.

"Portrait talks."

"Oh, yes, I keep forgetting about that."

Tremble's mind briefly drifted to the possibility of having a talk with the portrait of someone from her past. She longed to be able to do that with her father.

Inezia opened the large box in front of her. She pulled out a long chain with a pendant at the bottom. It was a butterfly.

"The Neverwrong Butterflies." Tremble whispered to Laken. He nodded.

One by one, Inezia pulled out a pendant. Each one was a different color, a different shape, a different combination of jewels. All were intricately beautiful. The ones for the girls were soft and delicate. The versions for the boys were manly. The last two she gave out were out of birth order by Tremble's observation. She looked at Laken, but found that his expression did not seem to indicate that he noticed this.

"Amadeus, I shall admonish you to take extra care to not lose this. The outcome of your life may depend on it."

Tremble would have sworn that Inezia glanced in her direction as she said those words. She shook off the feeling and continued to listen.

"My dear, Perpetua, you shall be a leader in this family. This pendant shall protect generations of your daughters. It will carry with it the strength I see in your young heart."

Inezia held Perpetua's pendant in clear view before she placed it around the young girl's next. The pendant around Tremble's neck vibrated causing her to reach for it. The two pendants were one in the same.

"Oh, this was Perpetua's? It is one of the Neverwrong Butterflies?" Tremble's eyes told Laken more of the feeling in her heart than did her words.

"It is. Now you understand its power and significance. Now you understand its protection. It has the magic of Inezia and all those strong women who have worn it since, including Jasmine."

"My children, there is no mistaking this—great evil shall invade this family. It shall come from the land that your parents and I fled. It shall also come from within yourselves. The only protection you will truly have is the strength within your hearts, the love that binds you, and the magic that these pendants hold. Hold tight to all of these things. Pass them down to the generations after you. One day, they may fight for your very lives."

Perpetua took hold of the butterfly that hung from the chain around her neck. The same one pulsated and glowed around Tremble's. Sensing that something was about to happen, Tremble took hold of Laken's hand. In an instant, their journey took them through time again.

"Do you feel again like we are falling?"

Tremble was not sure how long had passed as she and Laken made the next transition. Just after she had taken Laken's hand, she had suddenly felt very tired. She thought that she had dozed off in sleep during the weightless movement.

"This is a very strange feeling. As soon as you took my hand, I think I went to sleep."

"I was thinking the same thing. It was like we passed through a field of poppies." Tremble could not stop herself from giggling as the words left her mouth.

"What? I don't understand."

"Oh, Laken, I must give you a serious lesson in the childhood stories of the mortal world." Tremble squeezed his hand. "I just can't explain this feeling. We are falling into who knows what and where, yet, I feel so safe."

"You now better understand that you are not just protected by me. You are protected by generations of enchanters who are sending you the strength to do what they could not."

"And, what is that?"

"You shall overcome the evil that has shadowed their entire existence."

The words hit Tremble hard. In the same moment, her feet hit something hard as well. It was such a jolt that it caused her to release Laken's hand. She sat where she landed and did not move as her eyes adjusted to the new environment. There was fog all around. As it began to part, she saw that she was in a garden. Tremble felt around her. She had landed on something made of stone. As she turned around to see what was behind her, Tremble let out a scream as a stone hand was reaching toward her from behind. The rest of the stone body came into view. It was Claudia.

"We are in the Garden of Stone, Tremble. I realize this is frightening. Please try to stay calm and as quiet as you can." Laken's whispered words travelled with the fog to her. She slowly looked around. He was not in her field of vision.

"Where are you?"

"I'm just a few feet away. I think we should be still a moment to see if anything happens. I'm surprised that we have not had any further messages or instructions."

"Can those be sent to us as we travel to another time?" Tremble slowly slid her body away from the stone figure of her grandmother from generations before. Claudia's outstretched hand and her pained expression was unnerving close up.

"I would assume so. Now that you mention it, I am not sure. It may be that our journey has been set in motion and that it must play out as planned."

Tremble watched as Laken came into view. He was limping.

"In other words, we are on our own." Tremble let out a slight snort. "Somehow, this does not surprise me. Why are you limping?"

"I hit the ground hard. I jammed my ankle in the process. Nothing major."

As she rose to walk toward him, she saw that someone was heading toward them from the wooded area behind Laken. Tremble grabbed hold of his arm and drew him away from the statue as the person approached. It was Amadeus. Another person, who she could not completely see yet, was following behind him.

"I have to do it. It is the only chance we have to get them back."

"Amadeus. I said no. This is not the way, it is too dangerous."

It was Inezia behind him. Tremble watched as Amadeus took off his pendant and placed it on the reaching stone hand of his mother. Inezia was still a few feet behind him as dark smoke swirled around Amadeus.

Tremble felt Laken's arms around her pulling her back as she rose to rush to help Amadeus. His grip around her was stronger than she imagined as he literally pulled her backward and off her feet.

"You cannot change this." Tremble felt his breath on her ear as he calmly whispered to her. "Stay here with me. It's okay."

Tears welled in Tremble's eyes. It was like watching someone die. The blackness engulfed the young boy. A golden glow left his body and darkness took its place. When the blackness again disappeared, Amadeus was physically the same. As he turned toward them, toward Inezia, they saw that his eyes now were black and lifeless.

"Oh, my sweet child."

Inezia walked toward Amadeus. As she reached him, he pushed her away and walked toward the area where Tremble and Laken were sitting.

"You! YOU! You shall not overcome me."

For a brief moment, Amadeus stared right into Tremble's eyes as he spoke before quickly turning and directing his rage toward Inezia. Laken's grip was like a steel vice around Tremble.

"Your magic is not strong enough for me. I shall crush your pitiful charm under my feet."

Amadeus reached for the pendant that still hung from his mother's stone hand.

"Look at it, Tremble. Look at the pendant."

Laken's words directed Tremble's eyes at something that was obviously visible but hard to perceive at the same time. No longer was the glistening silver as it had once been, the pendant was now solid black. Every stone, every intricate portion of detail was dark as coal, dark as Amadeus' heart had been turned.

Before Amadeus could reach it, Inezia struggled to grab it.

"I cannot reverse what has transpired. The evil within you must lurk deep inside your heart. My magic will not work on you now. It shall however protect those who have loved you." Inezia held the pendant up just inches from his waiting hand. "One day, this shall come back to you. The giver of it shall free you from the bonds that hold you now."

Amadeus lunged for Inezia. As he did, the woman disappeared. They watched as Amadeus searched all around to find the woman. Finally, he walked back toward the area where the stone statues of his parents stood. He reached out and touched his mother's hand. Tremble saw some blackness leave his body. He looked again like a little boy, a lost little boy.

"I don't know what's happening to me." Tears flowed from his face.

Again, Tremble felt Laken pull her closer. She had not even realized that her body had once again tried to take her to the child.

"Why am I drawn to help him? It is his evil that has brought me here."

"Your souls are connected, in this life and in others. You are bound to each other—good and evil entwined."

Laken's words caused Tremble to turn around and face him. Again, she saw his eyes glow the emerald green she had seen before. Tremble began to understand and her heart froze with fear and sadness.

Chapter Eleven

"WAKE UP, CHILDREN. Wake up."

Tremble could hear a voice, but her eyes did not want to cooperate.

"Tremble, your rest is over. Open your eyes."

Slowly, she opened one eye. The view was blurry and bright. Opening the other eye only intensified what she had already surmised. Tremble slowly rose up on one arm. Her elbow went into something soft.

"Ouch!"

The softness was Laken's stomach. They were lying on the ground in the garden. Someone was standing above.

"Yes, that's right. You must get up. We have to go now."

Tremble shielded her eyes from the brightness that appeared to be coming from the sun. Only, it was not a golden light that was shining down, it was a bright blue light. More soothing than the sun of the world she had grown up in, with the same intensity and heat. The sky was yellow and the sun was blue. She must be in Neverwrong.

She moved out of the way, as Laken began to rise as well. Tremble noticed that the grass underneath was purple. Touching it, she realized that it had the very same texture.

"I do love the purple grass."

"It is delightful, isn't it?" The voice was speaking again. "So much more interesting than that green stuff you find in the mortal world."

"Earth is a green planet." Laken was now talking.

"That Earth is. This Earth is purple. It's royal." The voice laughed and Laken joined her.

"Who are you talking to? This blue light shining in my face is interfering with my vision."

Laken rose beside Tremble and helped her up off the ground. The person who had been speaking walked closer to them.

"I believe that this is Inezia."

"Laken is correct, my dear. I am Inezia."

The woman bowed. As she rose back up, Tremble began to see her more clearly. As the images she had seen previously alluded to, Inezia was a petite woman in stature. She was dressed in a long flowing gown of a deep teal blue. It was simple in design, yet elegant in style. What the woman lacked in height, she made up for in demeanor and presence. As Tremble had already ascertained, the woman took up the whole room.

"You were Inezia?" Tremble did not edit her shock.

"I am. My existence is still in the present tense, even though my physical self has not been seen for quite some time."

"I beg your pardon, ma'am. I meant no disrespect." Tremble bowed toward the woman as she apologized. "My knowledge of your existence period is only in the last hours, so forgive me for seeming abrupt."

"Oh, glitter poo, my dear; I do not need your apologies." Tremble and Laken both burst out laughing. "What? Why do you laugh so? It was not my intent to be humorous."

"Well, you said 'glitter poo.'"

Hearing Tremble say the words made another chuckle leave Laken.

"What is wrong with glitter poo? I suppose I could say something more rugged, but no matter the circumstance, I am still a lady. You will do well to remember that. Your royal manners will soon be on display for all of the subjects of Neverwrong to see. You shall even sooner have to show them to your beautiful mother, so straighten up."

"My mother?"

"Yes, my dear. I presented my likeness on that strange apparatus that the two of you are carrying. Did that not give you a clue that I might be leading you to our dear Jasmine?"

Tremble ignored the question and went on with one of her own.

"Do I understand that you have not been seen in all these years since what we just saw with Amadeus?"

"That is correct. I do like it when you get to the point. We have no time for dilly dally crock." This time, Tremble merely shook her head. The woman had some unusual expressions. "I have been in seclusion." Inezia shook her head and sighed. "The truth of the matter is that early on I was in mourning. I was consumed with grief and guilt. Look what happened to these two precious ones." The woman pointed to the stone statues. "They have been suspended in this horrible state for longer than I want to remember."

"Suspended?" Laken interrupted her story. "I thought it was

determined that they were killed and these were merely left as a reminder."

"That would be easier on the mind and heart, wouldn't it, young man?" Inezia tilted her head and looked up at Laken. "It would be much easier for the children and their descendants to live with it. The reality might be far different."

Laken and Tremble remained silent as they watched Inezia walk between the two stone statues. Tremble felt a pang in her heart as she considered the alternative to death that the woman was suggesting.

"Just because I have been in seclusion does not mean that I am ignorant to what has transpired in this family through the years. My magic is in those pendants." Inezia pointed to Tremble. "It makes me privy to what has gone on. I know that Amadeus was left behind in his mountain home and that his siblings forged a new life in a kingdom of their own creation. These dear ones here, his parents, were left as well. It is because of the evil that caused all of this. It is not right. It is not just. It is understandable. Those precious young minds and hearts could only take so much. I do not even begrudge what Baldric did to his only brother."

Tremble started to speak. Laken grasped her arm and shook his head for her to stop.

"Baldric saw what the others could not. Even Perpetua, as strong and as wise as she was even from youth, refused to see the evil that had penetrated Amadeus' soul. The poor lad should have died. It would have been a kindness graced upon him. Kindness was not something that he ever felt again after this dreadful day." Inezia pointed to the statues. For a moment, she seemed lost in some past thought. "We should have known better than to think we could flee the evil. You can run, but you cannot hide. Evil will follow you until you confront it. You are going to learn this, my dear. If you haven't already." Inezia turned toward Tremble.

"Is that why Scordato banished his siblings to an eternity within those portraits?"

"Amadeus was a young boy who had been kissed by evil. He was imprisoned in his family's former home. I am sure it was a life of frightening solitude. It was a fertile ground for the destruction of what goodness remained in him. His transformation to Scordato sealed the fate of his siblings and those who would descend from them. As powerful as he has become, he could not wage a war with all of them at once. He would have been defeated. It was the knowledge that he gained from the years he spent in the Library. That is what gave him the ancient tools he needed to seal their fate—their eternal imprisonment."

Inezia paused and moved to a bench nearby the statues. The weight of recounting all of the details seemed to tire her. Laken used this gap to ask his own question.

"How did Scordato get his siblings to all come back to their home in the mountain?"

"A very good question that is, Laken. You have spent your time wisely as you have learned your duties." Inezia smiled for a moment before she continued. "He used the power of the butterfly pendants."

"I thought he did not have his any longer. What we saw earlier showed that you retrieved it?"

"That is correct, Tremble. He still could harness the power of it because the core of its power remained in the Library. Come here." Tremble walked over to Inezia. The woman took hold of the butterfly portion of the pendant. She held it with both hands. "Show us your home."

A screen appeared before them with a view of the Library.

Tremble watched as the view grew smaller and smaller as it focused on one portion of the room. It was in a far corner away from the bookcases. On a table, next to a straight back chair, sat a beautiful glass globe. As the view became even more focused, Tremble saw that within the globe were butterflies—the same butterflies that had adorned the necks of all of the Royal siblings.

"I created eight pendants and eight matching globes. Those were for each of the children. Scordato figured out that this one was a homing device of sorts. I created it not knowing what the future would hold. It was for Claudia and Marcellus so that they could always have the ability to summon their children. I never dreamed that any of my creations would be used for evil. It was all created to be a protection."

Inezia let go of the pendant. Everything they had been viewing disappeared. The woman looked exhausted. Tremble knelt down in front of her.

"I have one more question then. Why has this pendant been given to me?"

"Because it is time for you to do what is right. You are never wrong when you do what is right."

The voice was that of an angel. It was soft and strong, a whisper of strength. Tremble froze and she held her breath. Looking into Inezia's eyes, she saw tears. The woman was nodding as she clasped Tremble's hands.

"Turn around, my child. It's time for you to meet your mother."

Drawing from the strength of this woman who was virtually a stranger to her, Tremble held tight to Inezia's hands as she slowly rose. The woman then rose with her and engulfed her in a hug as she whispered in Tremble's ear.

"This is for Dana. She says it is time. Be brave."

Tremble took a deep breath and looked up in the sky. The strange blue sun was shining in the strange yellow sky. As they touched, a green ring was around the sun. For a brief second, she let her nervous mind rest and wondered why the reverse did not cause a green ring in the world in which she had grown up.

"Turn around."

Inezia gave Tremble a little push. As she began turning, she felt like she was doing so in slow motion. Tremble saw all the trees around her and the flowers floating by. She saw a little animal scamper on the ground, carrying something in its mouth. Laken came into view. His face was full of excitement. A broad smile greeted her with a wink that said everything would be okay.

When the turn was complete, Tremble caught her breath as, for the first time, in the life she could remember, she saw Jasmine, face-to-face. At that moment, she fully understood what magic was. Tremble felt it pulsing through her veins as the woman who had given birth to her stood before her. It did not matter that she was a stranger by sight; they were connected by an energy that defied explanation.

For an instant, Tremble again saw the image she had first seen just a day or two previously. The colors around Jasmine were a mixture of fuchsia and red, purple and blue. At first, it appeared as if the woman's face was cracking. Jasmine was emerging from a wall. The wall that had separated them for twenty-one years. The layers were so close to her face that it gave the illusion that it was her own skin. In a blink, the illusion was gone. Tremble studied the real Jasmine's features. Her raven hair cascaded over her shoulders in soft circles. A sapphire colored ribbon held her hair at the nape of her neck. The ribbon matched the shimmering pantsuit Jasmine wore. The outfit complimented the striking eyes that glistened in a puddle of tears. As strong as Jasmine had been for those many years, she now appeared no longer able to hold back her emotions.

"I've waited a long time for this moment." Despite her emotion, Jasmine's voice was still strong. Tremble liked that. "I do not expect an instant relationship. I do not have the right to that. But, may I hold you in my arms?"

Tremble walked toward Jasmine. It was only a few feet, yet it seemed like miles. Her mind was spinning. Her mouth was dry. A surge of magic pulsated through her body. Tremble felt the serious of the moment, as an adult should. She felt the giddiness of anticipation, as only a child could.

When she reached her, Tremble noticed that they were the same height. Jasmine opened her arms and Tremble leaned into the embrace.

"I have waited so long for this moment." Jasmine whispered as the sobs she could no longer hold came.

"So have I."

Tremble whispered back, letting her own emotions flow returning the strong embrace she felt. After a few moments, the two released each other and stood back.

"I knew that I could not have found two better people in both our worlds to raise you." Jasmine beamed as she stared at her daughter. "They loved you from the first moment I spoke of you. I wish so much that Andrew was still here to know the young woman you have become."

Tremble's emotions were too jagged to allow her to respond. The moment—as it followed the previous hours, days, and weeks—was too much for her. She needed silence to gather the strength for what would come next.

Chapter Twelve

"I HAVE THOUGHT of a million questions that I wanted to ask you over the past few weeks." Tremble sat across from Jasmine on a patch of grass a short distance from the stone statues. "Now that you are here right in front of me, my mind is racing too much to think of any of them."

"Oh, my dear, I understand. I have a list of questions that is twenty-one years long."

Tremble was surprised at the ease she felt in the presence of the woman. A total stranger in many ways and yet someone she had always known. It was quite certainly a contradiction beyond imagination.

"I did what I had to do, Tremble. I would do it again to insure your well-being. Make no mistake though, it was the hardest thing I have ever done. It was not something that Forrest willingly agreed to. He is a warrior. He wanted to fight. I am a healer. I could not stand the thought of you being in harm's way."

Jasmine paused. It gave Tremble a moment to notice the small details of her behavior. She hoped that over time she could learn the little traits and behaviors that made Jasmine the woman she was.

"All of it is so grandiose. A few weeks ago, my biggest worry was being late for work. Now, my thoughts are consumed by a prophecy that I have yet to even hear in its entirety."

"No matter where your life is or what your obstacles may be, it always seems as if we do not know the whole story. Perhaps, it is that searching for knowledge that keeps us going."

Tremble thought for a moment about what Jasmine had said.

"Since no one seems to want to answer the big questions, maybe I shall just offer small ones. Why did you name me Tremble? It is such a strange name."

"Oh, my daughter, you think it is strange because no one else you know has such? You grew up in a world where uniqueness is superficially praised, yet, it is not truly revered. Perhaps, Laken has told you that in our world no one has the same name. We celebrate the individuality of every being that is born and adorn it with its own special monogram."

Jasmine looked off into the distance. Tremble longed for the mind-reading skills that others possessed. Yet, she realized that her mother's thoughts, at this moment, were probably more private than she dare hear.

"Have you ever been so happy that your inside feelings and your outside movements just make you shake with excitement? From the time we were small children, that is how it was when your father and I were together. We would tremble with delight to be together—to play, to discover, to learn. It did not matter what we were doing as long as we could do it together. It only made sense that the child that our union created should carry a name that symbolized how we felt. Your father and I chose your name because it so completely described our love."

"That's a wonderful explanation. I feel a little guilty now for wishing for a name everyone else had. Now, I still might wish for a more normal future life."

"I understand that. However, you must remember sometimes great opportunities come out of the most troublesome situations. As challenging as the days and weeks ahead will be, there could be something on the other side that is beyond your heart's desire. All of those twenty-one years were long and worrisome, but today is one of the most wonderful days of my life. It is a dream come true."

Jasmine pulled Tremble into an embrace. For the first time, Tremble felt the magic of her mother's love. It was easy for her to understand and appreciate Dana's love; Tremble had felt it every day of her life. Her mind could not imagine that there was another person out there who could give her a love that was equal to that. She felt it now in Jasmine's embrace. Love held captive for so long had a distinctive power all its own. As Jasmine released her, Tremble continued the conversation.

"CeCe and Belladonna have told me some things about your life. I have heard very little about Forrest. Tell me about him."

Tremble watched as Jasmine's face lit up. There was so much love showing in her eyes. Jasmine took hold of Tremble's hand.

"You have his hands. So many of your features I recognize as my own, but your hands are definitely just like your father's. His fingers are long and slender as yours are."

Jasmine paused and rubbed her hand over Tremble's. It made Tremble wonder if she was imagining holding Forrest's hand.

"To many, Forrest seems very stern and regimented. As a descendant of Baldric, those traits are in his nature. He was groomed to be a soldier, a leader in the Neverwrong military. However, in his early years of adulthood, he allowed his own interests to guide his life. He is an inventor, a man of technology."

"What types of things has he invented?"

"Oh, my, that list is long."

With a flick of her wrist, Jasmine brought into view a screen as Tremble had seen many times.

"Every time someone tries to explain something to me, a screen appears."

"Well, Tremble, you can thank your father for that. He developed this magical technology."

"Really?"

Tremble glanced over at Laken who was still within listening distance. He gave her a big smile and shook his head affirmatively.

"He thought that there needed to be a way for us to easily and clearly be able to view all of these memories we had extracted from our ancestors. The Seven's memories were long and detailed. They needed to be studied and logged."

"Because of the prophecy?"

"Yes, that was important. There are many other reasons as well. Queen Perpetua, for example, had a lifetime of intricate healing spells that future generations could benefit from knowing."

Jasmine paused as a handsome young man appeared on the screen. It appeared that he might have been in a laboratory-like setting as other men were surrounding him as they worked on a machine of some sort.

"That is Forrest shortly after we were married. He and his team were working on a piece of magical technology that would allow for an object to instantly be sent from one world to another."

"Like some sort of shipping device?"

"Yes, I suppose. He created it after I was talking one evening over dinner about how I wished for a quick way to send some of our medicine to other magical kingdoms. A healer from another kingdom had consulted with me that day regarding an ailment that one of her patients had. It was critical in nature. I had a potion that I could send her, but no quick way of getting it to her."

"Couldn't you just magically go there?"

"Yes, I could. The distance to this particular kingdom was quite far and the journey would have taken a while. Not everything is the snap of a finger with magic."

Tremble and Jasmine were silent for a few moments as they watched the screen. Forrest and his associates were diligently working on an unusual looking apparatus. After a few minutes of tinkering, the others stood back as Forrest appeared to begin a complicated spell. His hand movements were very elaborate. The scene caused Tremble to chuckle and look at Jasmine. She was smiling as well and shaking her head. At the end of his complicated delivery, there was a small puff of smoke and then nothing. Forrest and his team walked closer to it. A horrible noise erupted from the contraption followed by a huge cloud of green smoke. When the dust settled, they all looked like they had grass stains on their faces. Jasmine put her arm around Tremble and they howled with laughter.

"Oh, that was hilarious!"

"Yes, it was his first attempt. He finally conquered it after about a dozen of these types of mishaps. The device works perfectly now and is used throughout the magical universe for a variety of different purposes. Sadly, it was his last invention."

"Why is that? Did he decide to do something else?"

"No." Jasmine hesitated for a moment before continuing. "You were born. Our lives changed."

Jasmine's answer shocked Tremble. Even though, in the back of her mind, she knew that Jasmine and Forrest had both gone into hiding, she had not fully grasped that the lives they had both been living ceased.

"That's awful. All of the work that the two of you could have done. The wonderful inventions he could have created. The people you could have healed. I had not thought about how much in limbo your lives became. All because of me."

"My dear, do not fret over this. I daresay that both your father and I have had time to make a world of discoveries in our minds. We hope to have the opportunity to make them realities when we are all on the other side of this journey, together."

Tremble saw a pained look arise on Jasmine's face. It was the same type of look that Dana had just a few days ago when Tremble left. It was a look of hope laced with uncertainty and fear. Tremble knew how that look felt.

A few minutes of uncomfortable silence passed before Laken came over to where they were setting and began to speak.

"Your Royal Highness, if I may be so bold as to ask you a question."

Laken bowed his head in Jasmine's direction. Tremble wondered what he was going to ask.

"You may."

"I am sure that Tremble would like to know, as would the subjects of Neverwrong, where you have been hidden all of these years?"

Tremble shifted her gaze to Jasmine. As if the weight of the question was too much for her, the woman sat down.

"I have been here. I have lived in the Garden of Stone."

"How is it that you have gone undetected? Belladonna has persistently had the armies engaged in the search for you?"

"Only those who wish to be found can be found, young man." Inezia joined them from where she had been resting and interceded into the conversation. "Jasmine has been here with me. Our protection within this place has been the evil that is in its very soil and the sadness that permeates everything that grows here."

"I don't understand what you mean." Tremble's voice found the strength to speak.

"We are enchanters; our magic is what feeds us. It is a light on a dark day. Here in this garden, evil has staked claim. The darkness hides the light."

"So you mean that by surrounding yourself with evil, you both have become invisible."

"That is correct. I have hidden here for a couple of hundred years now. This smart girl found me when she was still a child." Inezia put her arm around Jasmine. "She kept my secret until she had a secret of her own to keep."

"How were you able to find Inezia here if all this darkness was hiding her?" Tremble looked from Jasmine to Inezia. She saw a soft smile pass between them.

"All my life, I have been able to see into the souls of others. I cannot explain it. I suspect though that, as my daughter, you understand this. I can see it in you." Tremble nodded. "When we were children, Belladonna, Forest, Xavier, Anton, and I would come here and explore. It was a forbidden place. Our parents knew there were dangers lurking here. They did not wish us to find them. To our rebellious nature, it was all we needed to hear. Our curiosity won over our obedience. We came frequently throughout those years. It was a place of happiness and great sadness. The others ignored any darkness that they might have felt here. I pursued it. I studied it. I opened my heart to it. I am a healer—I thought I could fix it."

"Her open heart called out to my sad one. I had lived here for the entire history of Neverwrong. I had a bird's eye view of what transpired with those born of the original ones. Through those pendants, I watched the generations pass. Their stories flew back to me on the wings of the butterflies."

"After I left you with Dana and Andrew, I wandered from place to place in the mortal world for a while. Then, one day, the necklace you wear now, lit up. It frightened me. However, it also made me remember the woman who had created it. I decided that perhaps she was the one who could best help me. I felt that the one who had taken care of the original royal children could surely protect me."

"Wait a minute. If this necklace came to life, who was it that made that happen?" Tremble suspected that she already knew the answer.

"It was Inezia."

"But, I thought that Scordato possessed the globe that was the homing device for all these."

"Oh, he does. I was the creator of all of them though." Inezia's words were full of delight. "I possess the power to call them forth without the globe. It is but a tool. My magic is what controls all of them."

"And, do you still possess the pendant that belonged to Amadeus?" Laken's question caught Tremble off-guard.

"I do. It was overcome with evil as was Amadeus."

"What shall become of it, then?"

"Only love can reverse the evil that is within it. An act of love caused Amadeus to forsake the protection of the pendant.

An act of love could reverse all that it has come in contact with.'

"More. Still more prophecy to heap on the head of the heir." Tremble walked away from them and toward the stone statues. "Would not Marcellus and Claudia wish that they had never come to this land?"

"The prophecies do intertwine. It is true." Jasmine spoke as Tremble walked away. "You should remember though that these are layers in a complicated story. The obvious conclusion to this story may not be how it ends. You asked a question. You asked why you received the pendant. It is a part of your heritage. The pendant passes to the first born in each successive generation. There is actually another pendant that would pass to you as well—the pendant that your father now wears."

"These pendants combined will have the power to defeat the magic that is locked deep inside the dark pendant that was Amadeus'."

"I still don't understand." Tremble turned toward Inezia. "You possess that pendant. How can the magic be harmful? You've had it for hundreds of years."

"The magic is still within it. The evil that took Marcellus and Claudia is the same evil that consumed young Amadeus. The pendant could still exert its power by his possession or that of his firstborn. Unfortunately, I cannot undo that."

"But, he does not have an heir." All eyes went to Laken.

"Yes, he does." Jasmine darted her eyes to Inezia as she spoke. A sick feeling came over Tremble.

"Why have we never seen this person? Surely, Belladonna would have known and would have prepared me—"

"Belladonna does not know." Jasmine paused and looked directly at Tremble. "She suspects, but she does not know it for a certainty. This heir came into existence through trickery and deception."

"No, I don't think that is possible. It just cannot be."

Tremble, Jasmine, and Inezia watched as Laken began walking backwards toward the statues.

"Amadeus, in the form of Scordato, has an heir, a firstborn son." Inezia stood next to Jasmine. "His existence changes everything."

"Please say this is not true." Laken continued to walk backward. "I think this is a trick, Tremble. Something is not right here."

Tremble began to walk toward him. Jasmine reached for Tremble's arm to pull her back. She shrugged out of her grasp.

"Laken, you know it in your heart. Haven't you always known it?" Inezia's words were calm.

"No, I was created to be the Protector of the heir to Neverwrong. It has been my entire life. I cannot be—"

"Laken, it is true." Inezia spoke the words clearly. "You are the first born son of Scordato."

"Stop it!" Tremble screamed. "This is ridiculous. His life was created in a laboratory."

"Tremble, you know it. You've known it in your heart for some time."

Jasmine's words hit Tremble hard. As she looked up, she saw the hurt that crossed Laken's face.

"Is that why you didn't trust me? You knew that I came from a monster?"

"Laken, do not say that." Jasmine's voice was calm again, reassuring. "It was a trick. Belladonna was tricked. Scordato got into the lab. He made a switch. You must not be fearful. Remember, Scordato was Amadeus. He was as pure as any member of The Seven. The evil that has consumed him has made him dark.

You can fight that."

"Can I? His seed was not taken from a child. It was not taken from Amadeus. If this is true, I was created with the DNA of Scordato. Would not the evil reach those genes?"

Laken stopped and stood in front of the stone statues of Marcellus and Claudia. Their pained expressions were amplified by the horror that was on Laken's face.

"Give me the pendant." Laken reached out to Inezia.

"What? I don't think—" The words tumbled out of Inezia's mouth. She shot a look at Jasmine.

"Laken that will not prove anything." Jasmine's voice was calm. She reached out her hand to him. "Come and sit down. We will talk about this. You are the Protector. You have been so good to—"

"No! There will always be doubt. I heard it in Belladonna's voice the night before we left. She tried to warn Tremble. She knew what I was." Laken looked Tremble squarely in the eye. "I will never harm Tremble. I must find a way to never harm Tremble."

Tremble's eyes filled with tears as she saw the terror crossing over him. He looked as if he was warring within himself.

"Give me the pendant. Let me prove that this is all a mistake. It is probably another trick of Scordato. This is a diversion. He wants you to be fearful of me while he does something else. It's all his evil." Laken's eyes darted back and forth between all of them. "If I am not his heir, nothing should happen when I put the pendant on, right? Right, Inezia? I should not be affected if I am not his heir."

"No, nothing should happen. But, the evil within it is still very strong."

"Yes, but you have carried it around all of these years, have you not? It has not affected you, has it? You originated the magic. If there was harm to be had, I would think it would come to you."

"Laken, it is not the best way to prove—"

"No, Inezia, I think he is right." Tremble spoke up. She caught Laken's eye and heard a silent 'thank you' in her head. "Scordato is the only one who really knows. The rest is speculation. Even a DNA test would not prove it, as we know that Laken would have partial Royal genetics either way. Maybe he is right. This could be just a decoy created by Scordato. It could be a diversion for him to do something. He and the evil one want me to be suspicious of my own Protector."

"Tremble, what if it is true?" Jasmine stood between Laken and Tremble. "What if this proves that Laken is the heir of Scordato?"

Tremble looked from Jasmine to Laken. The depth of their communication at that moment was even unfathomable to her.

"Then, we will work our family problems out. We will heal him."

Tears welled up in Laken's eyes. He looked down at the ground. While he was doing so, Tremble looked at Jasmine. Her mother shook her head.

"We've got to find out. Eventually. There's no other alternative."

"We could send Laken away." Laken's head rose as Inezia spoke.

"I am the Protector of the heir of Neverwrong. I would rather die than to not fulfill my duties."

"Enough of this." Inezia walked toward Laken. "He has the right to know."

She pulled a long dark chain from her pocket. On it hung

an equally dark version of a butterfly. It looked like it had been through a fire. She imagined that dealing with such evil could make anything appear as if it had faced a tormenting flame.

Tremble held her breath as Inezia held the pendant out to Laken. She felt Jasmine's arm reach around her. Laken looked down at the chain, and then into Tremble's eyes.

"Whatever happens, please remember me as your loyal servant. That is all my heart has ever wanted to be."

"No, I will remember you as my friend. You shall be my friend for all of the days of my life. That does not stop now. It cannot."

Laken's smile was broad and beautiful. It reminded Tremble of when they had met that first night in her home. Tremble held her breath as she watched Laken reach and take the pendant out of Inezia's hand. Nothing happened when he touched it. He looked up at Inezia. Her expression was blank.

"You'll have to put it on."

Tremble watched as Laken held it in his hands for a moment. He briefly looked at her before he slowly put the chain over his head and let the pendant rest on his chest.

For a moment, nothing happened. Then, slowly, gradually, where the blackness had been, silver returned. The butterfly began to shimmer with the green coloring that had originally been. It was again as beautiful and detailed as the one that hung around Tremble's own neck.

Laken looked up at Inezia. The woman had a shocked look on her face.

"Inezia, what do you think this means?" Jasmine released her hold on Tremble and walked toward Laken.

"I don't know. I think it must mean that Laken does indeed have a connection to Scordato or Amadeus. Perhaps it is that he embodies the good that was in the child who originally wore it." Inezia paused. Tremble saw a look of happiness begin to cross Laken's face as Inezia resumed speaking. "I did not expect to ever see the pendant back to its original beauty. It hasn't been this way since—"

"Since Marcellus and Claudia were turned into these statues." Laken turned toward the stone figures. "Maybe I am the antidote to that. Maybe my loyalty and love for Tremble, for the Royal Family can undo all of the wrong that was done so many years ago."

Before anyone knew what he was doing, Laken turned and reached out to the figure of Claudia. He had just about reached her outstretched hand when a scream came out of Tremble that she did not know was inside her.

"NO LAKEN, DON'T DO IT!"

Her plea was too late. She watched as if in slow motion Laken began to turn to stone. It started with the hand that had touched Claudia's and soon encompassed his whole body.

Tremble crumbled to the ground as she watched in horror. The image of the young Amadeus passed before her eyes as she now had glimpsed what he had experienced so long ago.

SHE DID NOT KNOW how much time had passed. Jasmine and Inezia had joined Tremble in her crumbled state. Like balloons with their air released, the three were lifeless and silent as they grasped what they had just witnessed.

Jasmine rose first. She did not look at her daughter as she walked toward what were now three statues of stone. Tremble watched with vacant eyes as Jasmine examined Laken's now stone silhouette from behind before she walked around to the front.

Tremble bowed her head and held it in her hands. She began to rock back and forth. She could no longer look at the stone version of her friend.

"Inezia, come here, you must see this."

The woman looked the several hundred years that she must have been as she slowly rose to join Jasmine. Tremble watched the look of surprise cross Inezia's face as the woman gazed at the front of Laken.

"I do not understand it. That is amazing."

Tremble's curiosity gave her the energy she needed to rise and walk toward them. Her eyes immediately went toward Laken's face. It broke her heart to see his broad smile frozen in stone. He had so much hope in that last moment, so much hope to help everyone.

"Can you imagine what it might mean?" Jasmine's question took Tremble back to whatever was amazing the women.

"What are you two talking about?"

Jasmine pointed her finger at the pendant around Laken's neck. It was not stone as the rest of him. The pendant was still intact as it had been when he first put it on. The silver chain was lying around his neck of stone with the beautiful green jewels of the pendant glistening on his chest.

"I don't understand." Tremble looked at Inezia.

"For some reason, the evil could not take it this time." Inezia walked around to examine the entire chain. Tremble and Jasmine did the same. It was all in its original form.

"Do you think we should take it off of him?" For some reason, Jasmine's question startled Tremble. It gave her an uneasy feeling.

"No!" Tremble said as she saw Inezia begin to reach for it.

"I don't know why. I know clearly though that we should not take it off him. It will break the spell if we do." Tremble paused and looked at her mother. "Maybe this is protecting him in some way."

"Tremble, I'm afraid that Laken is beyond our protection."

"Maybe that is true, Jasmine. But just because he is beyond our protection does not mean he is completely beyond any protection. I think Tremble is right. We shall leave it, at least for the time being."

Tremble walked around and around the three statues. As she did so, she fingered the butterfly that was around her own neck. Her thoughts whirled in all sorts of different directions. She replayed all that had transpired over the previous few weeks. It whisked through her memory like a rewinding video. All of a sudden, she stopped and looked at Jasmine.

"Do you know where Forrest is?"

"Not really. I have suspected that Scordato may be holding him in this very garden. He has been able to communicate with me a few times. I know that he communicated with you. He has been careful to do it in such a manner so that Scordato cannot intercept it and find you."

"That was a waste of his effort."

A shocked look crossed Jasmine's face.

"Scordato has always been around me, even from the time I was a small child. As recent as the day that Laken first appeared to me and as far back as when my father purchased my dog Choo Choo, Scordato has been as close to me as you are right now."

"I don't understand. We had guardians there at all times."

"He doesn't want to hurt me, not like that. He wants me ready for battle. Scordato wants a worthy opponent. I had to grow up and come into my magic to be a challenge to him."

Jasmine stared off in the distance in shock.

"You mean I could have had all these years with you. I didn't have to hide you."

"I don't know about that. I really do not. He has never tried to hurt me though. I'm sure all that is about to change." Tremble paused and looked again at Laken. "We've got to find Forrest. I think that having his pendant may be the key to overthrowing Scordato and, even more importantly, all the evil that came before him."

"I do not know how you will find him. The armies of Neverwrong and our allies around us have searched for Forrest for years. It's like searching for a needle in a haystack."

Tremble stared deeply into the eyes of the stone Laken. She thought of all that she had learned about her heritage. The vast history of Neverwrong was complicated and simple at the same time. She knew that the answer to all that was happening was probably hiding in plain sight. The answer was there. After a few moments, a smile crossed her face.

"Perhaps someone from a different world would have more success. Perhaps it will take someone made of something else entirely to find the one who was left behind." Tremble paused and her smile grew broader. "I think I know just the person for the job."

ACKNOWLEDGEMENTS

Many fiction writers will tell you that they are driven to write. A group of characters and a storyline is inside them dying to get out. I would agree with that and offer another thought. I believe that some of us are born to be storytellers. I find myself telling stories in all aspects of my life. Those who are closest to me in my personal and career lives would agree. I cannot just talk about a topic. Eventually, the conversation turns into a story.

Because of this, I must first offer my thanks to my readers. Those wonderful people, near and far, who fall in love with my characters and take the journey as well. I can say that I would write anyway. Many stories fill my file cabinets and hard drives, never published, to prove that point. Yet, I know that many of these adventures would just stay in my head if I did not know that there were kind souls waiting to read them. Thank you, my readers, my friends, for helping me get those voices out of my head.

It takes a special person to be brave enough to review the work of a friend. I am fortunate to have several such friends in my life. I am always learning something from Pam Newberry. As a lifelong educator, Pam has a gentle way of showing me where my writing has gone astray. She reels me back in with the proverbial tap on the back of the head and in the process helps me to become a better writer. I have told her that I do not want to publish a book without her critique. I sincerely hope that I never have to do that. Take some time to check out her stories at www. pambnewberry.com.

God did not give me a sister, instead He gave me a Marcella. I do not believe I have ever met someone who enjoys reading more or who can so quickly read a book and glean the entire story. Marcella Taylor and I met in our newspaper reporting days and have formed a friendship that I cannot imagine could ever end. Her encouragement is one of the things I value most.

One of the smartest things I did while writing the Legends of Graham Mansion series was to recruit Donna Stroupe to be the series' primary editor. Not much gets past Donna. She might even say that she has been able to slowly change my aversion to commas. Her love of a good story also makes her editing even more valuable as she reads like a reader as well as an editor.

I entrust Carole Bybee with the task of being my final reader before a book is published. Carole combs through the "non-sense" and gives a final red pen to the grammar, spelling, and clarity. Then, she also adds some insight into what intrigued her most about the characters or plot and askes some very specific questions that force me to think as my readers will. I am very grateful for the role she plays in fine-tuning the story.

I knew that I was going to like Cassy Roop when I heard the name of her company—Pink Ink Designs (www.pinkindesigns. com). What I have since learned is that she is a consummate professional who can take an old graphic designer's (me) cryptic ideas and bring them to life. Her covers are works of art and her formatting skills are stellar. I am pleased that she is on Team Enchanted Journey.

A silent strength and constant in my life is my husband. He never complains that I am spending too much time writing, even when I most certainly am. I have promised him a big boat if I ever write a best seller. Maybe if I keep typing, he can one day go on his own magical journey.

ABOUT THE AUTHOR

Rosa Lee Jude began creating her own imaginary worlds at an early age. While her career path has included stints in journalism, marketing, hospitality & tourism and local government, she is most at home at a keyboard spinning yarns of fiction and creative non-fiction. She lives in the beautiful mountains of Southwest Virginia with her patient husband and very spoiled rescue dog.

The Enchanted Journey is Rosa Lee's second series. She is also the co-author of the award-winning time-travel series, the Legends of Graham Mansion. Learn more about her writing life at RosaLeeJude.com.